Captain Lesbee began to build up mental pictures of a nonmechanical civilization that would be dazzled and dominated by the tremendous and wonderful ship from Earth. He had visions of himself walking among the awed creatures like a god come down from the sky.

That vision ended forever on the ninth day after the orbit was established, when a general warning was sounded from every speaker on the ship.

"This is Captain Lesbee. Observers have just reported sighting a superspaceship entering the atmosphere below us. The direction the ship was traveling indicates that it must have passed within a few miles of us, and that we were seen.

"All officers and men will therefore take up battle stations.

"I will keep you informed."

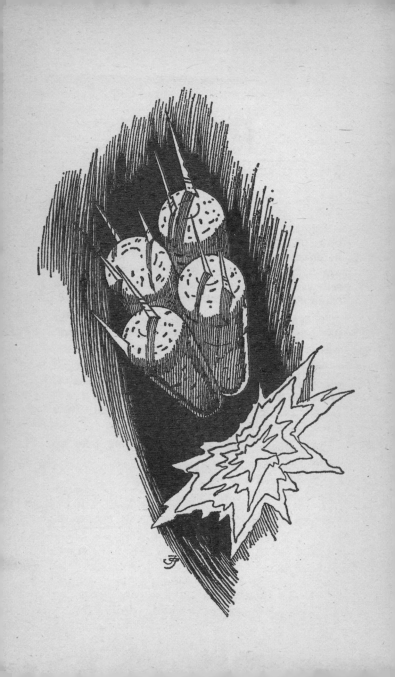

ROGUE SHIP

A. E. VAN VOGT

DAW BOOKS, INC.
DONALD A. WOLLHEIM, PUBLISHER

1633 Broadway
New York, N.Y. 10019

PUBLISHED BY
THE NEW AMERICAN LIBRARY
OF CANADA LIMITED

Cover art by Greg Theakston

FIRST DAW PRINTING, MAY 1980

1 2 3 4 5 6 7 8 9

DAW **sf**
BOOKS

DAW TRADEMARK REGISTERED
U.S. PAT. OFF. MARCA
REGISTRADA. HECHO EN U.S.A.

PRINTED IN CANADA
COVER PRINTED IN U.S.A.

DEDICATION

For Ford McCormack, friend, logician, technical expert, man of many parts, who seems to be as much at home in the exotic universe of translight-speeds as on the stage of important little theaters—to whom I am indebted for some of the concepts and for nearly all of what is scientifically exact in this fantastic story.

1

Out of the corner of one eye, young Lesbee saw Ganarette climbing the steps that led to the spaceship's bridge. He felt vaguely annoyed. Ganarette, at nineteen, was a big, husky youth with a square jaw and belligerent manner. Like Lesbee himself, he had been born on the ship. As a nonofficer, he was not allowed on the bridge and it was that, entirely aside from his own personal dislike of Ganarette, that annoyed Lesbee about the intrusion.

Besides, he was scheduled to go off duty in five minutes.

Ganarette mounted the final step, and climbed gingerly down to the cushiony floor. He must have been intent on his descent, for when he looked up and saw the black, starry heavens, he gasped and then stood teetering a dozen feet from Lesbee, staring into the darkness. His reaction startled Lesbee. It hadn't struck him before, but there were actually people on this ship whose only view of space had been by way of the visiscreen.

The sheer, stark reality of the plastiglass bridge, with its effect of standing there in the dark, empty space itself, must be mind-staggering. Lesbee had a vague feeling of superiority. He had been allowed on the bridge since early childhood.

To him, what was out there seemed as natural and ordinary as the ship itself.

He saw that Ganarette was recovering from his initial shock. "So," Ganarette said, "this is what it's really like. Which is Centaurus?"

Stiffly, Lesbee pointed out the very bright star which was visible beyond the sight lines of the astrogation devices. Since nonmilitary personnel were never permitted on the bridge, he wondered if he were obligated to report the youth's intrusion.

He felt reluctant to do so, first of all because it might antagonize the other young people aboard. As the captain's son, he was already being treated as a person set apart. If he definitely aligned himself with the ship authority, he might find himself even more cut off.

He had a sudden mental picture of himself repeating his father's lonely existence.

He shook his head ever so slightly, silently rejecting that way of life.

In a few minutes his period of duty for the day would be over. At that point he would lead Ganarette gently but firmly down the steps and give him as friendly a warning as possible. He saw that the youth was looking at him with a faint, cynical smile.

"Doesn't look very close. Boy, they sure pulled a trick on the colonists, pretending the ship was going to make the trip at the speed of light or faster and get there in four years." Ganarette's tone was sarcastic.

"Nine more years," Lesbee said, "and we'll be there."

"Yeah!" Cynically. "That I have to see." He broke off. "And which is Earth?"

Lesbee led him to the other side of the bridge to a sighting device that was always aimed at Earth's sun.

The pale star held Ganarette's interest for nearly a minute. His face changed; gloom was written there. He slumped a little, then whispered, "It's so far away, so very far away. If we started back now, you and I would be forty years old when we got there."

He whirled and firmly grasped Lesbee's shoulders. "Think of it!" he said. "Forty years old. Half of our lifetime gone, but still a chance to have a little fun—if we turned back this instant."

Lesbee freed himself from the clamping fingers. He was disturbed. It was more than a year since he had heard that kind of talk from any of the younger folk. Ever since his father initiated the lectures on the importance of this, the second voyage to Alpha Centauri, the wilder spirits among the young people had quieted down.

Ganarette seemed to realize that his action had been foolish. He stepped back with a sheepish grin. Once more he became satiric. He said, "But of course it would be silly to turn back now when we're only nine years from Centaurus, a mere eighteen years farther from Earth, there and return."

Lesbee did not ask, return to what? Long ago, most of those aboard had ceased to regard the original purpose of the voyage as having meaning. There was the sun, wasn't there, with no visible change? And so there must be an Earth to return to. Lesbee knew that among the young people his father was considered to be an old fool who dared not go back to face the ridicule of his fellow scientists. The pride of this foolish old man was continuing to force a shipload of people to spend the equivalent of a normal lifetime in space. Lesbee had often felt the horror at such a prospect that Ganarette was now expressing, and he could not help but share some of the condemnation of his father.

Trembling, he looked at his watch. He was relieved to see that it was time to switch on the automatic pilot. His duty period was over. He turned, manipulated the control switches, counted the lights that went on, cross-checked with the two physicists in the engine room, and then, as he always did, made a second count of the lights. They were still exactly right.

For twelve hours now, electronic machinery would guide the ship. Then Carson would assume the watch for six hours. The first officer would be followed, after twelve more hours, by the second officer who, in turn, would be succeeded by Browne, the third officer. And then, when still another twelve hours of automatic flight had gone by, it would be his turn again.

Such was the pattern of his life, and so it had been since his fourteenth birthday. It was certainly not a hard existence. The ship's top officers actually had an easy time of it. But each man was jealous of his duty stint, and always showed up on the dot. A few years ago, Browne had even had himself wheeled to the upper deck in a wheel chair and then assisted to the bridge by his son, who had remained with his sick father during the entire six hours.

Such devotion to duty puzzled young Lesbee, and so he had made one of his rare efforts to communicate with his father, asking him what could have motivated Browne. The old man smiled at him quizzically, and explained, "Going on watch is the status symbol of every officer, so don't ever regard it lightly. They don't, as Browne is demonstrating. We are the official ruling class, my boy. Treat all those men with respect, use their formal titles, and in return they'll recognize your status. Whatever benefits accrue to the nobility aboard this ship will depend on how well we maintain such amenities."

Lesbee had already discovered that several of the benefits

were that the prettiest girls smiled at him, and came running when he smiled back.

Recalling the smiles of one girl in particular, he emerged from his reverie and realized that he would barely have time to wash up before the movie started.

He grew aware that Ganarette was looking at the clock on the low-built control board. The young man faced Lesbee. "O.K., John," he said, "you might as well get it now. Five minutes after the motion picture starts my group is taking over the ship. We intend to make you captain, but only on the condition that you agree to turn back to Earth. We won't hurt any of the old fogies—if they behave. If they act up, there'll be as much trouble as they want. If you try to warn anybody, we shall reconsider our plan to make you captain."

Ignoring Lesbee's dumfounded reaction, he went on, "Our problem is to make sure that we don't do anything that might arouse suspicion. That means everybody, including you, should carry on as always. What do you normally do when you leave the bridge?"

"I go to my quarters and wash up," said Lesbee, truthfully.

He was beginning to recover from the enormous shock of the other man's pronouncement. He grew aware that he was in a state of anguish, and that amazingly what he felt was an awful anxiety that "these fools"—he muttered the words under his breath—would somehow mess up their mutiny, and this mad voyage would continue on into infinity. As he realized his instant sympathy with the rebels, Lesbee swallowed, and abruptly felt confused.

Before he could recover, Ganarette said reluctantly, "All right—but I'll go with you."

"Maybe it'd be better if I skipped going home," said Lesbee doubtfully.

"And have your father become suspicious! Nothing doing!"

Lesbee was uneasy. He was, he realized, falling in with the plot. He sensed unknown dangers in that direction. Yet the emotion that had broken through from a hidden depth of his being, was still driving him on. He said in a conspiratorial tone, "That would be preferable to having him wonder what I'm doing with you. He doesn't like you."

"Oh, he doesn't!" Ganarette sounded belligerent, but suddenly he looked unsure of himself. "All right, we'll go straight down to the theater. But remember what I said.

Watch yourself. Be as surprised as the others, but be prepared to step in and take command."

He impulsively put his hand on Lesbee's arm. "We've got to win," he said. "My God, we've got to."

As they went down into the ship a minute later, Lesbee found that he was somehow tightening his muscles, bracing himself as for a struggle.

2

Lesbee sank into his seat. As he sat there, he grew aware that all around him in the theater, people were fumbling their way to their places. He had time for doubt, for second thought. If he was going to do anything, he would have to act swiftly.

Ganarette, who had been in the aisle whispering to another young man, crushed into the seat beside him. He leaned toward Lesbee. "Only a few minutes now, as soon as everybody is in. When the doors close, we'll let the lights go off and the picture get started. Then in the darkness I'll make my way to the stage. The moment the lights go on, you join me."

Lesbee nodded, but he was unhappy. Only a short time had gone by since the great rush of sympathy for the rebellion, but now that feeling was fading, replaced by an uneasy fear of consequences. He had no conscious picture of what might happen. It was an over-all and growing sense of doom.

A buzzer sounded. "Ah," whispered Ganarette "the picture is going to start."

The time was passing inexorably. The internal pressure to act was strong in Lesbee. He had a terrible conviction that he was ruining himself with the authority group aboard, and that on the other hand the mutineers merely intended to use him during the early stages of their rebellion, that later he would be discarded. Abruptly, he was convinced that he had nothing to gain by their victory.

In a sudden desperation, he stirred in his seat, and looked around tensely, wondering if he couldn't escape.

He gave that up after one quick look. His eyes had accustomed to the night of the theater and it wasn't really dark at all. Over to one side he could see Third Officer Browne and his wife sitting together. The older man caught his distracted gaze and nodded.

Lesbee grimaced an acknowledging smile, then turned away. Beside him, Ganarette said, "Where's Carson?"

It was Lesbee's seeking gaze that found First Officer Carson sitting near the back of the theater, and it was he who located the second officer slumped down in one of the seats near the front. Of the senior officers of the ship only Captain Lesbee himself had not yet arrived. That was a little disquieting but Lesbee took assurance from the fact that the theater had its normal packed appearance.

Three times a "week" there was a show. Three times a week the eight hundred people on the ship gathered in this room and gazed silently at the scenes of far-off Earth that glided over the screen. Seldom did anyone miss the show. His father would be along any minute.

Lesbee settled himself to the inevitability of what was about to happen. On the screen a light flickered, and then there was a burble of music. A voice said something about an "important trial," and then there were several panels of printed words and a list of technical experts. At that point Lesbee's mind and gaze wandered back to his father's reserved seat.

It was still empty.

The shock of that was not an ordinary sensation. It was an impact, astonishment mingled with a sense of imminent disaster, the sudden tremendous conviction that his father knew of the plot.

He felt his first disappointment. It was an anguish of bitter emotion, the realization that the trip would go on. His feelings caught him by surprise. He still hadn't realized the depth and intensity of his own frustration aboard this ship, seven thousand and eight hundred days out from Earth. He whirled to word-lash Ganarette for having made such a mess of the plot.

Lips parted, he hesitated. If the rebellion were destined to fail, it wouldn't do to have made a single favorable remark about it. With a sigh he settled back in his seat. The anger passed and he could feel the disappointment fading. Rising in its place was acceptance of the inevitability of the future.

On the screen somebody was standing before a jury and saying, ". . . the crime of this man is treason. The laws of Earth do not pause inside the stratosphere or at the moon or at Mars—"

Once again the words and the scene couldn't hold Lesbee. His gaze flashed to Captain Lesbee's seat. A sigh escaped from his lips as he saw that his father was in the act of sitting down. So he hadn't really suspected. His late arrival was a meaningless accident.

Within seconds the lights would flash on and the young rebels would take over the ship.

Curiously, now that there was no chance of his doing anything, he was able for the first time to give his attention to the motion picture. It was as if his mind were anxious to escape from the sense of guilt that was beginning to build up inside his body. He looked outside rather than in.

The scene was still a courtroom. A very pale young man was standing before a judge who wore a black cap, and the judge was saying, "Have you any final words before sentence is pronounced upon you?"

The reply was haltingly delivered: "Nothing, sir . . . except we were so far out. . . . It didn't seem as if we had any connection with Earth— After seven years, it just didn't seem possible that the laws of Earth had any meaning—"

It struck Lesbee that the theater was deathly quiet, and that the rebellion was many minutes overdue. It was then as he listened to the final words of the judge that he realized that there would be no rebellion, and why. The judge in that remote Earth court was saying:

"I have no alternative but to sentence you to death . . . for mutiny."

It was several hours later when Lesbee made his way to the projection room. "Hello, Mr. Jonathan," he said to the slim, middle-aged man who was busily putting away his cans.

Jonathan acknowledged the greeting politely. But his face showed wonder that the captain's son should have sought him out. His expression was a reminder to Lesbee that it didn't pay to neglect *any* one aboard a ship, not even people you considered unimportant.

"Odd picture you showed there at the beginning," he said casually.

"Yeah." The cans were being shoved into their protective cases. "Kind of surprised me when your dad phoned up and asked me to show it. Very old, you know. From the early days of interplanetary travel."

Lesbee did not trust himself to speak. He nodded, pretended to inspect the room, and then went out—scarcely looking where he was going.

For an hour he wandered around the ship and, gradually, a coherent purpose formed in his mind. He must see his father.

That was unique because he had not spoken to his father except in monosyllables since his mother's death.

3

He found the old man in the spacious living room of the apartment the two of them shared. At seventy-odd, John Lesbee had learned to keep his counsel, so he merely glanced up when his son entered, greeted him courteously, and resumed reading.

A minute went by before the father grew aware that his son had not gone on to his own bedroom. He glanced up again, surprised now. "Yes?" he said. "Anything I can do for you?"

Young Lesbee hesitated. A formless emotion was upon him, a desire to be at peace with the other. He had never forgiven his father for the death of his mother.

He said abruptly, "Dad, why did Mother kill herself?"

Captain Lesbee put down his book. He seemed suddenly paler, though the color was hard to judge on a face that was naturally gray-white. He drew a slow, deep breath. "We-e-l-ll," he said, "what a question!" His voice sounded breathless, and his eyes were bright.

"I think I should know," Lesbee persisted.

There was silence—that lengthened. The lined face of the old man continued to be colorless; his eyes remained unnaturally bright.

Lesbee II went on, "She used to talk to me in a bitter way, all against you, but I never understood it."

Captain Lesbee was nodding, half to himself. He seemed to have come to a decision, for he straightened. "I took advantage of her," he said evenly. "She was my ward, and as she grew older she became attractive to me as a woman and I felt desire. Under normal circumstances I should have kept such feelings to myself, and she would normally have gone off and married some young man of her own generation. But I convinced myself that she would at least be alive if she went with me. In this way, I betrayed her trust in me which was that of a child for a father and not that of a woman for her lover."

Since he had never thought of his mother as being particularly young, Lesbee II found it difficult to grasp that this was what had caused her to have such intense emotions. Yet he recognized that he had been given an honest statement. Nonetheless, it was a moment for all the truth, not just a part of it, and so he went on: "She used to call you stupid and"—he hesitated—"and other things. One thing you're not is stupid. But, sir, Mother swore to me that the death of Mr. Tellier was not an accident, as you said. She, uh, called you a murderer."

The color was creeping into his father's cheeks, an ever so faint flush. The old man sat for a long moment, smiling faintly. Then: "Only time will tell, Johnny, whether I'm a genius or a fool. I proved more than a match for Tellier but that was because he had to nerve himself for each step, and with my greater experience I could see what was coming next. Someday, I'll tell you about that long, drawn-out struggle. With his knowledge of the equipment aboard, he could have defeated me. But he was never quite as strongly motivated as I was."

He must have realized the explanation was too generalized, for he continued after only a moment: "I can explain it all in a few sentences. On takeoff, Tellier took it for granted that we would be able to attain very nearly the speed of light and so obtain the benefits predicted by the Lorentz-Fitzgerald Contraction Theory. We couldn't do it—as you know. The drive fell far short of Tellier's theoretical expectations. As soon as he realized that we were in for a long voyage, he wanted to turn back. Naturally, I couldn't let him do that. He thereupon went into a state of mind verging on the psychotic, and he was in that condition when he had his accident."

"Why would Mother hold that against you?"

The elder Lesbee shrugged. Something of that long-ago impatience he must have felt, thickened his voice as he said, "Your mother never did understand what Tellier and I were wrangling about, in terms of its scientific meaning. But she did know that he wanted to turn back. Since she wanted that also, she maintained that his knowledge as an astrophysicist was superior to mine as a mere astronomer, and that, therefore, I was stupidly opposing the views of a man who really knew the facts."

"I see." Young Lesbee was silent, then: "I've never understood the Lorentz-Fitzgerald Contraction Theory, nor what it was that you discovered about the sun that made you undertake this voyage."

The older man looked at him thoughtfully. "It's a long, involved idea," he said. "For example, it's not the sun itself but a warp in space which I analyzed. This warp should by now have caused the destruction of the solar system."

"But the sun didn't flare up."

"I never said it would," said his father in an irritated tone. He broke off: "My boy, you'll find my detailed report among the ship's scientific papers, and also available is Dr. Tellier's account of his experiments in attempting to reach high speed. His papers contain a description of the famous Lorentz-Fitzgerald Contraction Theory. Why don't you read it all when you have time."

The youth hesitated. He was not eager to hear a long, scientific account, particularly at this hour of the night. But he recognized that this communication with his father was taking place because he himself was in an overstimulated condition; it might be a one-time occurrence. And so, after a moment, he persisted: "But why didn't the ship speed up as predicted? What went wrong?"

He added quickly, "Oh, I realize lectures were given on the subject but, knowing you, I feel that they were what you wanted people to believe in the interests of the voyage. What's the truth?"

The old man's eyes twinkled suddenly, then he chuckled. "I really turned out to have a natural instinct for knowing how to maintain discipline and morale, didn't I?" He grew somber. "I wish I could inject some of that into you." He broke off. "But never mind. Your observation is correct. I told the people what I wanted them to think. The actual truth is substantially what I have already told you. When Tellier discovered that the ejected particles could not be speeded up to the point where they would expand, it became necessary to conserve our fuel supply. Theoretically, particles expanded to the level predicted for them at the velocity of light would have given us almost infinite power on a thimbleful of fuel. As it is, we used up hundreds of tons of fuel to get the ship up to 15 per cent of light-speed. Since by that time, we could calculate our fuel situation in terms of simple additive and subtractive arithmetic, I ordered the engines shut off. We've been coasting ever since at that speed. We'll have to use an equal amount of fuel tonnage to slow down when we get to Centaurus. If things work out when we arrive there, then, of course, no problem. But if they don't, then somewhere, sometime, we're going to pay the price for Tellier's failure."

"What price?" Lesbee II asked.

"No fuel," said his father laconically.

"Oh!"

"One more thing," said the old man. "I am perfectly aware that people believe there is still an Earth, despite my prediction, and that I am the subject of bitter criticism in this area. I thought this over years ago, and I decided it is better for me to suffer a loss of pride than to argue with them. Reason: my authority derives from Earth. If people actually came to believe that Earth had indeed been destroyed, then all of us in power—me, you, and the other officers—would no longer be able to do what I did tonight: remind dissidents what Earth does to those who disobey its mandate."

The youth was nodding. He felt reluctant to discuss this particular subject, and so it was time to end the conversation. There *was* another question in his mind, having to do with the relationship of the older Lesbee with Tellier's widow since his mother's death. But a moment's consideration convinced him that such an inquiry was not in order.

"Thanks, Dad," he said, and walked on to his room.

4

For weeks they had been slowing down. And, day by day, the bright stars in the blackness ahead grew larger and more dazzling. The four suns of Alpha Centauri no longer looked like one brilliant diamond, but were distinct units separated by noticeable gaps of black space.

They passed Proxima Centauri at a distance of over two billion miles. The faint red star slowly retreated behind them.

Not Proxima the red, the small, but Alpha A was their first destination. From far Earth itself, the shadow telescopes had picked out seven planets revolving around A. Surely, of seven planets, one would be habitable.

When the ship was still four billion miles from the main system, Lesbee II's six-year-old son came to him in the hydroponic gardens—where he had been called to settle a discussion on the uses of solid state coolants in growing vegetables and fruit.

"Grandfather wants to see you, Dad, in the captain's cabin."

Lesbee nodded, and noted that the boy ignored the workers in the gardens. He felt vaguely pleased. It was well for people to realize their station in life. And, ever since the boy's birth, several years after the crisis created by Ganarette, he had consciously striven to instill the proper awareness into the youngster.

The boy would grow up with that attitude of superiority so necessary to a commander.

Lesbee forgot that. He tugged the youngster along to the playground adjoining the residential section, then took an elevator to the officers' deck. His father, four physicists from the engineering department, and Mr. Carson, Mr. Henwick, and Mr. Browne were in conference as he entered. Lesbee sank quietly into a chair at the outer edge of the group, but he knew better than to ask questions.

18

It didn't take long to realize what was going on. The sparks. For days the ship had been moving along through what seemed to be a violent electric storm. The sparks spattered the outer hull from stem to stern. On the transparent bridge it had become necessary to wear dark glasses; the incessant fireflylike flares of light upset the muscular balance of the eyes, and caused strain and headache.

The manifestation was getting worse, not better.

"In my opinion," said the chief physicist, Mr. Plauck, "we have run into a gas cloud—as you know, space is not a total vacuum, but is occupied, particulary in and near star systems, by large numbers of free atoms and electrons. In such a complicated structure as is created by the Alpha A, B, C, and Proxima suns, gravity pull would draw enormous masses of gas atoms from the outer atmospheres of all the stars, and these would permeate all the surrounding space. As for the electrical aspects, apparently a disturbance, a flow, has been set up in these gas clouds, possibly even caused by our own passage, though that is unlikely. Interstellar electrical storms are not new."

He paused and glanced at one of his assistants questioningly. The man, a mousy individual named Kesser, said:

"It happens that I'm in disagreement with the electrical-storm theory, though I also agree on the presence of masses of gas. After all, that's old stuff in astronomy. But now—my explanation for the sparks. As long ago as the twentieth century, perhaps even earlier, it was theorized that the gas molecules and atoms floating in space readily interchanged velocity for heat or heat for velocity. The temperatures of these free particles, when such an interchange occurred, was found to be as high as twenty thousand degrees Fahrenheit."

He looked around, momentarily very unmouselike. "What would happen if a molecule traveling at such speed struck our ship? Sparks of heat, of course." He paused. He was a graying man with a hesitant way of speaking. "And then, of course, we must always remember the first Centaurus expedition and be doubly careful."

There was a chilled silence. It was strange but Lesbee II had the impression that, although everybody had been thinking of the first expedition, nobody wanted it mentioned.

Lesbee II glanced at his father. Captain Lesbee was frowning. The commander had grown more spare with years, but his six feet three inches still supported 175 pounds of bone and flesh. He said:

"It is taken for granted that we shall be cautious. One of the purposes of this voyage is to discover the fate of the first expedition." His gaze flashed toward the group of physicists. "As you know," he said, "that expedition set out for Alpha Centauri nearly seventy-five years ago. We are assuming that the engines would have kept going. Therefore, some control would have existed in any fall through the atmosphere of a planet, and a trace of its presence will remain. The question is, what would be operable after three quarters of a century?"

Lesbee was amazed at the various answers. There were so many things that the physicists expected would survive. The "pile" engines. All electronic detectors and many other energy sources. It was also noted that printed instruments could withstand 800 gravities. The shell of the ship? Its survival would depend on the velocity of the ship as it fell through the planet's atmosphere. It was theoretically possible that the speed would be vast beyond all safety limits. At such immense speeds, the entire machine would go up in a puff of heat energy.

But that was not that the experts anticipated. There should be something. "We should be able to trace the ship within hours of arriving at the planet where it crashed."

As the men got up to leave, Lesbee caught his father's signal for him to remain behind. When the others had gone, the older man said, "It is necessary to make plans against a second rebellion. There is a scheme afoot to evade our connection with Earth law by establishing a permanent colony on Centaurus and never returning to Earth. Since, as you know, in my view there is no Earth to go back to, this new development baffles me. It still seems to be in our favor that people do believe that Earth survives. But I must advise you that this time the rebels do not intend to make you captain. Let us, therefore, discuss tactics and strategy—"

5

Watch duty became a nightmare. The three chief officers and Lesbee divided it into three-hour shifts that ran consecutively. They wore semispace suits for protection when they were on the bridge, but Lesbee's eyes never stopped aching.

During his sleep period, he dreamed of sparks dancing with an unsteady beat under his eyelids, and there was a picture of a successful mutiny led by Ganarette, surprising them in spite of their preknowledge. It was miraculous that his father knew as much as he did about the plot.

The speed of the ship came down to interplanetary levels. And, slowly, they drew near the planet they had selected for a first landing. It was the only possible selection. Of the seven planets in the system, six had already been measured as being of Jupiter size; this seventh one had a diameter of ten thousand miles. At 120 million miles from Alpha A, a sun 15 per cent hotter than Sol, it almost approximated Earth conditions. There was the added complication of the pale but sun-sized star, Alpha B, visible in the blackness little more than a billion miles from Alpha A, and the almost invisible C, too, would have its effect. But that scarcely mattered beside the fact that here was a planet of approximately the right size, and even at a distance it glowed with a jewel-like atmosphere.

Orbiting at four thousand miles from the surface of the planet, the giant *Hope of Man* maintained a velocity befitting its closeness—and the preliminary study began of a planet that was instantly observed to have cities on it.

What should have been the thrill, literally, of a lifetime, was a fearful fight against mounting tension. The instruments on the bridge, and in the alternative control room, in their quiet way reported surface and atmospheric conditions at least partially unfavorable to human life. Yet it was understood by everyone that readings taken at a distance were only indicative.

21

Once, when Lesbee II accompanied his father to the bridge, aging chemist Kesser came dragging over. "The sooner we get down there into the atmosphere for the final testing, the better I'll like it," he said.

Lesbee II had the same feeling, but his father only shook his head. "You were just out of college, Mr. Kesser, when you signed up for the voyage. You have not that awareness of the standards of precaution by which we must act. That's the trouble aboard this ship. Those who were born during the trip will never begin to understand what efficiency is. I don't intend to inspect this planet directly for at least two weeks, possibly even longer."

As the days passed, the initial information was confirmed by new readings. The planet's atmosphere had a strong greenish tinge that was identified as chlorine. There was a great deal of oxygen in the stratosphere, and the comparison that everybody made was to a habitable Venus, but here masks would have to be worn against the irritating chlorine. Kesser and his assistants were uncertain about the exact composition of the hydrogen and nitrogen in the air below, but this merely increased their desire to go down and examine it.

At four thousand miles, the difference between water and land was sufficiently distinguishable for a photographic map to be made. Cameras, taking thousands of pictures a second, obtained a view entirely free of sparks.

There were four main continents, and uncountable islands. Fifty-nine hundred cities were large enough to show clearly, despite the distance. They were not lighted at night, but that could have been because there was no night in the Earth sense. When Alpha A was not shining down on the continents below, either Alpha B or Alpha C or both, were shedding some equivalent of daylight.

"We mustn't assume," said Captain Lesbee, in one of his daily talks on the intercoms, "that the civilization here has not discovered electricity. Individual lights in houses would not necessarily be visible if they weren't used often."

These talks, Lesbee discovered, did not serve the function that his father intended. There was a great deal of criticism, a feeling that the commander was becoming too cautious.

"Why don't we dive down," said one man, "collect some samples of the atmosphere, and end this uncertainty? If we can't breathe that stuff down there, let's find it out, and get started home."

In spite of his confidence in his father, Lesbee found himself sharing the sentiment. Surely, the people below would not take violent offense. And, besides, if they departed immediately—

Privately, his father told him that the mutiny had been called off pending developments. The rebel plan, to settle forever, was shaken by the possibility that the planet might not be suitable for human beings, and that, in any event, permission to settle would have to be secured from the present inhabitants.

"And though they won't admit it," said the commander, "they're afraid."

Lesbee was afraid, too. The idea of an alien civilization made his mind uneasy. He went around with an empty feeling in his stomach, and wondered if he looked as cowardly as he felt. There was only one satisfaction. He was not alone. Everywhere were pale, anxious faces and voices that quivered. At least he had his father's strong, confident voice to encourage him.

He began to build up pictures of a nonmechanical civilization that would be dazzled and dominated by the tremendous and wonderful ship from Earth. He had visions of himself walking among the awed creatures like a god come down from the sky.

That vision ended forever on the ninth day after the orbit was established, when a general warning was sounded from every speaker on the ship.

"This is Captain Lesbee. Observers have just reported sighting a superspaceship entering the atmosphere below us. The direction the ship was traveling indicates that it must have passed within a few miles of us, and that we were seen.

"All officers and men will therefore take up action stations.

"I will keep you informed."

6

Lesbee put on his suit, and climbed up to the bridge. The sparks were dancing like mad on the outside of the plasti-glass, and it was a pleasure to sit down at the bridge directive board and watch the screen that had been rigged up two days before by the physics department. The screen was fed frames by the high-speed scanners, but an electronic device eliminated every picture that had a spark on it. The speed of the pictures made the scene appear continuous and uninterrupted.

He was sitting there when, abruptly, there was a flash of brightness at the lower end of the screen—about ten miles away.

A ship!

It was instantly a matter for speculation as to how it had got within range so quickly. One second, the surrounding space was empty; the next second, a gigantic spaceship had hove to.

Captain Lesbee's voice came quietly from the speaker: "Apparently these beings have discovered a drive principle, and have inertia-defeating techniques, that enable them to dispense with gradual starts and stops. They must be able to attain interstellar maximum velocities within minutes of leaving their atmosphere."

Lesbee II scarcely heard. He was watching the alien vessel. He did remember thinking that it took the *Hope of Man* many months to accelerate and decelerate, but that thought quickly blanked out; the comparison was too unfavorable.

With a start he saw that the ship was larger. Closer.

Sharply, the commander's voice came: "Torpedo crews, load! But take warning! Any officer firing without orders will be punished. These people may be friendly."

Silence reigned on the bridge while the two vessels approached within two miles of each other. Both were now in the same orbit, the alien slightly behind the Earth ship but

24

evidently using power, for it was coming closer still. A mile, then half a mile. Lesbee licked dry lips. Distractedly, he glanced at First Officer Carson and saw that he was rigid in his chair, glaring into the screen. The man's bearded face showed that same stiff tension.

Again, Captain Lesbee's voice came on the speaker behind them: "I want all weapons officers to listen carefully. The following order applies only to Torpedo Chamber A, under the command of Technical Gunnery Mate Doud. Doud, I want you to ease out a disarmed torpedo. Understand me! Kick it out with compressed air."

Lesbee II saw the torpedo emerge, and heard his father's voice give more directions: "Ease it out several hundred yards, so they can't miss seeing it. Then keep it under radio control cruising around in a narrow area of about two hundred feet."

The commander explained quietly to his unseen audience: "My hope is that this action will apprise the other ship that we have weapons but are not using them in aggressive action. Their response may indicate whether or not their quiet approach was a friendly or a cunning one. It might also give us some information that we desire, but I won't develop on that at this moment. Do not be alarmed. All our screens are up. These consist of various types of repulsion energy fields. They represent Earth's mightiest science."

That was briefly reassuring. But the empty feeling came back to Lesbee II, as a hard, tense voice sounded on the speaker: "This is Gunnery Mate Doud. Somebody's trying to take the radio control of the torpedo away from me."

"Let them have it!" That was Captain Lesbee, quickly. "They've obviously discovered it is harmless."

Lesbee watched as the Earth torpedo was drawn toward the hull of the bigger ship. A door opened in the vessel's side, and the torpedo floated into it.

A minute passed; two; and then the torpedo emerged and slowly approached the *Hope of Man*.

Lesbee waited, but he didn't actually need words now. It was not the first time in these past days that something of the enormity of this meeting of the civilizations of different suns struck him. For some weeks now, the trip had had a new meaning for him, and there was also the wonder of his being on the scene. Of the multibillions of Earth-born men, he was here on the frontier of man's universe participating in the greatest event in the history of the human race. Suddenly, it seemed to him that he understood the pride his father took in this voyage.

For a moment, sitting there, his fear gone, Lesbee shared that pride, and felt a joy beyond any emotion he had ever known.

The feeling ended, as Captain Lesbee's voice came curtly: "I am limiting this call to officers and to the science department. I want, first, Doud, to try to take control of the torpedo. See if they'll let it go. Immediately."

There was a pause; then: "Got it, sir."

"Good." Captain Lesbee's voice sounded relieved. "How about the telemetry readout?"

"Loud and clear, both channels."

"Check the arm/disarm position monitors."

"Yes, sir. Negative all around. Disarmed."

"They hardly had time to rig those." The captain was still cautious. "Any abnormal readings? Excess radiation?"

"Negative. Radiometers normal."

7

The trial of Ganarette began shortly after the breakfast hour on the following sidereal day. The *Hope of Man* was still in her orbit around Alpha A-4, but the alien machine had disappeared. And so the people of the ship could devote themselves to the trial itself.

The extent of the evidence startled Lesbee II. Hour after hour, records of conversations were reeled off, conversations in which Ganarette's voice came out sharp and clear, but whoever answered was blurred and unrecognizable.

"I have followed this policy," Captain Lesbee explained to the silent spectators, "because Ganarette is the leader. No one but I will ever know the identity of the other men, and it is my intention to forget, and act as if they did not participate."

The records were damning. How they had been recorded,

Lesbee could only guess, but they had caught Ganarette when he believed he was absolutely safe. The man had talked wildly on occasion about killing anybody who opposed them, and a dozen times he had advocated the murder of the captain, the two chief officers, and Lesbee's son. "They'll have to be put of the way, or they'll make trouble. The sheep on this ship just take it for granted that the Lesbees do the bossing."

Emile Gamarette laughed at that point, then he stared boldly at the spectators. "It's the truth, isn't it?" he said. "You bunch of idiots take it for granted that somebody can be rightfully appointed to boss you for your entire lives. Wake up, fools! You've got only one life. Don't let one man tell you how to live it."

Ganarette made no effort to deny the charge. "Sure, it's true. Since when did you become God? I was born on this ship without being asked whether or not I wanted to live here. I recognize no rights of anybody to tell me what to do."

Several times he expressed puzzlement that was slowly growing in Lesbee II's own mind. "What is this all about?" he asked. "This trial is silly, now that we've discovered the Centaurus system is inhabited. I'm fully prepared to go back to Earth like a good little boy. It's bad enough to know that the trip was for nothing, and that I'll be sixty years old when we get back. But the point is, I do recognize the necessity now of going back. And besides, there was no mutiny. You can't try me for shooting off my face when nothing actually happened."

Toward the end, Lesbee watched his father's face. There was an expression there that he did not understand, a grimness that chilled him, a purpose that did not actually consider evidence except as a means to a hidden end.

When dinner was less than a hour away, the commander asked the accused a final question: "Emile Ganarette, have you entered your complete defense?"

The big-boned young man shrugged. "Yeah. I'm through."

There was silence, then slowly Captain Lesbee began his judgment. He dwelt on the aspects of naval law involved in the charge of "incitement to mutiny." For ten minutes, he read from a document that Lesbee had never seen before, which his father called the "Articles of Authority on the *Hope of Man*," a special decree issued by the elected cabinet of the Combined Western Powers a few days before the ship's departure from its orbit around Earth:

" '. . . It is taken for granted that a spaceship is always an appendage of the civilization from which it derives. Its personnel cannot be considered to have or be permitted to exercise independent sovereignty under any circumstances. The authority of its duly appointed officers and the assigned purposes of its mission are not alterable by elective process on the part of its personnel at large. A spaceship is dispatched by its owners or by a sovereign government. . . . Its officers are appointed. It is governed by rules and regulations set up by the Space Authority.

" 'For the record, it is therefore here set down that the owner of the *Hope of Man* is Averill Hewitt, his heirs, and assignees. Because of its stated destination and purpose, his ship is given sanction to operate as a military vessel, and its duly appointed officers are herewith authorized to represent Earth in any contact with foreign powers of other star systems, and to act in every way as representatives of the armed forces. There are no qualifications to this status—' "

There was much more, but that was the gist. The laws of a remote lifetime-distant planet applied aboard the spaceship.

And still Lesbee had no idea where his father was pointing his words. Or even why the trial was being held, now that the danger of mutiny was over.

The final words fell upon the audience and the prisoner like a thunderbolt:

"By right of the power vested in me by the people of Earth through their lawful government, I am compelled to pass judgment upon this unfortunate young man. The law is fixed. I have no alternative but to sentence him to death in the atomic converter. May God have mercy on his soul."

Ganarette was on his feet. His face was the color of lead. "You fool!" he quavered. "What do you think you're doing?" The deadliness of the sentence must have sunk in deeper, for he shouted: "There's something wrong. He's got something up his sleeve. He knows something we don't know. He—"

Lesbee had already caught his father's signal. At that point, he and Browne and Carson, and three special MPs, hustled Ganarette out of the room. He was glad of the chance for movement. It made thinking unnecesary.

Ganarette grew bolder as they moved along the corridors, and some of his color came back. "You won't get away with this!" he said loudly. "My friends will rescue me. Where are you taking me, anyway?"

It was a wonder that had already struck Lesbee. Once more, the quick-minded Ganarette realized the truth in a flash of insight. "You monsters!" he gasped. "You're not going to kill me *now?*"

The vague thought came to Lesbee that an outsider would have had difficulty distinguishing between prisoner and captors by the amount of color in their cheeks. Everyone was as pale as death. When Captain Lesbee arrived a few minutes later, his leathery face was almost white, but his voice was calm and cold and purposeful. "Emile Ganarette, you have one minute to make your peace with your God. . . ."

The execution was announced just before the sleep period, but long enough after dinner to prevent physical upset.

Lesbee had not eaten dinner. Nor had any of the other executioners.

8

Lesbee awakened the following day from his uneasy sleep to the realization that his "call" alarm was buzzing softly.

He dressed, and headed immediately for the bridge.

As he sank into the seat beside Browne, he noted with surprise that the planet, which had been so close, was nowhere to be seen. A glance at the mighty sun, Alpha A, brought another, more pleasant surprise. It was receding, already much smaller. The three suns A, B, and C were still not a unit, but only one, the dim C, was still ahead; the other two swam like small, bright lights in the blackness behind them.

"Ah," said Captain Lesbee's voice from behind them. "There you are, John. Good morning, gentlemen."

They looked around. The commander, looking rested, walked over to a chair and sat down.

Lesbee acknowledged the greeting diffidently. He was not too pleased at the attempt at friendliness, and was no longer sure that he liked his father. However wildly Ganarette might have talked at times, it was hard to forget that they had grown up together. Besides, Ganarette had been right! Once the threat of mutiny was past, it was hardly the time to execute. The finale had come too quickly, Lesbee thought agonizingly. Given a chance to consider the sentence, he himself might have protested to his father. The unseemly haste of the execution repelled him. The cruelty of it shocked him.

His father was speaking again: "While you slept, John, I had a specially equipped torpedo projected into the atmosphere of A-4. I'm sure that everyone here would like to see what happened to it."

He did not wait for a reply. The picture on the screen changed. It showed a scene, recorded earlier, with the planet looming quite close, and off to one side a bright gleam where the torpedo was falling toward the haze of atmosphere below.

What happened then was surprising. The torpedo began to twist and dive in a random fashion; a wisp and then a trail of smoke issued from it.

"Another minute and we would have lost it altogether," said Captain Lesbee. "I'm surprised the recall command got through, but it did."

The scene showed the torpedo as it slowly straightened its course, turned, and climbed back toward the ship. Part of the return journey was through a heavy rain flooding down on the eerie land below.

The torpedo rocketed to the vicinity of the ship, and was snatched by tractor beams and drawn aboard.

As the picture on the screen faded, Captain Lesbee climbed to his feet and approached a long, canvas-covered object, which Lesbee had noticed when he first entered the bridge.

Very deliberately, the commander tugged the canvas aside.

It took a moment for Lesbee to recognize the scarred and battered cigar-shaped thing that lay there, as the once-glistening torpedo.

Involuntarily, he approached it, and stared down at it in amazement. There were shocked murmurs from some of the other men. He paid no attention. The inch-thick hull of the torpedo was seared through in a dozen places as if by intolerable fire. Behind him, a man said hesitantly:

"You mean, sir that . . . atmosphere . . . down . . . there—?"

"This torpedo," said Captain Lesbee, as if he had not heard the question, "and possibly the *Centaurus I*, ran into a hydrochloric acid and nitric acid rain. A ship made of glass, platinum, or lead, or covered with wax, could go down into an atmosphere capable of that kind of precipitation. And *we* could do it if we had a method of spraying our ship continuously with sodium hydroxide or other equally strong base. But that would take care of only one aspect of the devil's atmosphere down there."

He looked around again, gravely now. "Well, that's about all, gentlemen. There are other details, but I need scarcely point out that this planet is not for human beings. We shall never know if the first Centaurus expedition went down into that atmosphere without proper investigation. If they did, they discovered the truth the hard way."

The words lifted young Lesbee out of his tension. He had taken it for granted they would spend several years in exploration. Now instead, they would be going home.

He would see Earth before he died.

The excitement of that thought ended, as his father spoke again: "Whatever the civilization of the aliens, they were not very friendly. They warned us, but that could be because they had no desire for our big ship to come crashing down on one of their towns. The warning transmitted, they departed. Since then, we have seen two ships come up and disappear, apparently heading out to interstellar space. Neither of the ships made any effort to approach us."

He broke off, added: "Now, let me turn to another matter. The inhabitants of this system are evidently psychologists, for they sent along film strips of life on their planet. Their assumption, I presume, was that we would be curious, and so during the next few days we shall show these films. I have taken a peek, and I'll just say that they look like walking snakes, very tall, very graceful, sinuous, and intelligent. It must be a pleasurable and elegant existence that they live, for there is an atmosphere of extreme gentility."

He paused, then gravely: "I hope you are as convinced as I am that there is nothing for us here. However, *we are not going home*.

"For two reasons—first, that Earth is no longer a habitable planet was certainly one of my considerations. But I'll say no more about that, in view of my personal involvement. The other reason is, suppose there is an undamaged Earth—then we are bound to continue on. My orders from Averill Hewitt, the owner of this ship, are to proceed to Sirius, then Procyon.

"You can see why it was necessary to eliminate the troublemaker in our midst. The example made of him will restrain the hotheads."

The intensity went out of his voice. He finished quietly: "Gentlemen, you have all necessary information. You will conduct yourselves with that decorum and confidence which is the mark of an officer, regardless of the situation in which he finds himself.

"You have my best wishes—"

9

John Lesbee III, acting captain, sat in the great captain's chair, which he had rigged up on the bridge, and pondered the problem of the old people.

There were too many of them. They ate too much. They required constant attention. It was ridiculous having seventy-nine people aboard who were over a hundred years old.

On the other hand, some of those old scoundrels knew more about science and interstellar navigation than all the younger people put together. And they were aware of it, too, the cunning, senile wretches. Which ones could be killed without danger of destroying valuable knowledge? He began to write down names, mostly of women and nonofficers among the men. When it was finished he stared down at it thoughtfully, and mentally selected the first five victims. Then he pressed a button beside his chair.

Presently, a heavily built young man climbed up the steps from below. "Yeah," he said, "what is it?"

Lesbee III gazed at the other with carefully concealed distaste. There was a coarseness about Atkins that offended his sensibilities, and in a curious fashion it seemed to him that he could never like the man who had killed his father, John Lesbee II, even though he himself had ordered the killing.

Lesbee sighed. Life was a constant adaptation to the reality of inorganic and organic matter that made up one's environment. In order to get a man properly murdered, you had to have a capable murderer. From a very early age he had realized that his nonentity of a father would have to be eliminated. Accordingly, he had cultivated Atkins. The man must be kept in his place, of course.

"Atkins," said Lesbee with a weary wave of one hand, "I have some names here for you. Be careful. The deaths must appear natural, or I shall disown you as an inefficient fool."

The big man grunted. He was a grandson of one of the original workers in the gardens, and it had caused quite a stir when he had been relieved of his duties as a gardener some years before.

The resentment died quickly when the officer's son who protested the loudest was put to work in Atkins' place. Lesbee III had thought out things like that long before he acted against his father. His plan was to kill Atkins as soon as the man had served his purpose.

With an aloof air, he gave the first five names, gave them verbally; then, as Atkins withdrew down the steps, he turned his attention to the screen. He pressed another button, and presently the graying son of the old first officer climbed up to the bridge and came over to him, slowly.

"What is it—Captain?"

Lesbee hesitated. He was not sure he liked the slight pause before the use of his title. He was not sure he liked Carson. He sighed. Life was a problem of *so many* adjustments, with everybody making a fetish of hoarding what knowledge they had. One had to put up with so much, and that was strange because he could remember in his own youth that people then had been much more openhanded and openhearted.

Why, the first generation had taught their children everything they knew—so it was said.

"Uh, Mr. Carson, what are the latest reports on Sirius?"

Carson brightened. "We are now within ten thousand million miles. The ship has been swung around for deceleration purposes, but it will be a week yet before the telescopes will be able to determine definitely the size of the plants or whether they have atmospheres."

"Any, uh, radiation activity?"

Mr. Carson started to shake his head. He stopped: A curious expression came into his eyes. Lesbee twisted to follow his gaze.

Slowly, he stiffened.

The forward half of the plastiglass bridge was twinkling with a scattering of sparks. Even as Lesbee stared, they grew more numerous.

In an hour the gas storm had closed in around them.

Sirius A at five hundred million miles looked about the size of the sun as seen from Earth. Lesbee III did not make the comparison from his own experience. There were motion-picture views that provided a fairly exact standard for judgment. What was radically different was the planetary arrangement.

There were two planets between Sirius A and its companion sun. The one nearest B was very close to its star and had a correspondingly high speed. The other one, which was four hundred and seventy million miles from A, moved more sedately around its large, brilliant sun.

It was this nearest planet that offered their only hope. With a diameter of seventeen thousand miles, it was less than half the size of the second planet, and about one hundredth the size of the planets that swung weightily beyond the erratic orbit of Sirius B. Through the clouds of Sirius A-1, cities were visible.

Lesbee III studied the reports, and looked at the scene below, depressed but determined. It was clear that the universe had not been designed for the comfort and convenience of man. But he must be careful not to accept the implied defeat. Reluctantly, he made his way to the cabin where, for long now, he had isolated his aged grandfather.

He found his grandfather sitting in a chair, watching a small screen view of the planet that swung nearer and nearer. Possession of the screen was one of the many small courtesies which the younger man extended to the other, but so far it had produced no friendliness. His grandfather did not look up as he entered. Lesbee hesitated, then walked over and settled himself in a chair facing the old man.

He waited. It was hard when people misunderstood one's purposes. He had once thought his grandfather would understand even if no one else did, that John Lesbee III had the interests of the trip at heart.

Perhaps it was too much to expect, though. Human beings were always willing to be objective—about other human beings; and so an old man resented the method by which he had been retired. Some day, no doubt, he, Lesbee III, would be retired by Lesbee IV, now ten years old. It seemed to the young man, in a sudden burst of self-pity, that when the time came, he would accept the situation gracefully—provided it didn't happen too soon.

His annoyance passed. He launched his bombshell. "Grandfather, I have come to ask your permission to announce that you will come out of retirement during the whole period in which we are in the vicinity of Sirius, and that during that period you will direct the activities of the ship."

The long, thin body moved, but that was all. Lesbee suppressed a smile. It seemed to him that his grandfather's mind must be working furiously. He pressed his purpose, as persuasively as possible: "Throughout your life, sir, you have had but one purpose: To ensure that the voyage of the *Hope of Man* is completed. I know what your feeling is. After all, I'm the person who actually decided to accept the ship as a permanent home." He shrugged. "Before this, people kept wanting to go home. I've stopped all that and I've urged everyone to accept life here and now. People used to be worried about the fact that there was one more girl in the third generation than there were men. I solved that problem very simply. I took a second wife. It was shocking for a while, but now no one gives it a thought." He leaned back easily. "A voyage like this is something special. We're a little, private world, and we have to make private adjustments to changing conditions. I was hoping to have your approval of all this."

He paused, and waited. Still the old man said nothing. Lesbee smothered his irritation with an affable smile. "You might be interested, sir, in the suggestion I have to make for our stay in the Sirius system. Naturally, it is already pretty certain that we cannot land here. That atmosphere below is saturated with sulfur. Just what that would do to our ship, I don't know. But one thing is certain. We've got to find out right here where we go next."

It seemed to Lesbee that he had his audience interested now. The old man was stroking his scraggly white beard, his lips were pursed.

But again it was Lesbee who had to break the silence: "I have studied the reports of the methods used in trying to establish communication with the Centaurians. The methods all seem too timid, considered in retrospect. There was no bold determination on your part to force attention from them, and although you spent months longer than your original intention, cruising around, your lack of initiative made that merely a waste of time. Certainly the nature of the atmosphere, which you discovered there, entitled you to believe that it was a chlorine-breathing, interstellar civilization somewhat superior to that of Earth. Now, here seems to be a sulfur-breathing world."

He leaned forward with a sudden intensity. "We must make ourselves so obnoxious to the inhabitants of this planet of Sirius A that they will give us all the information we want. Are you interested?"

The old man stirred. Slowly he straightened his long body. His eyes narrowed to slits of blue. "Just what have you got in mind," he asked, "besides murder?"

10

The atomic bomb that was fired into the atmosphere of Sirius A-1, attained a velocity of thirty miles a minute. And so, in spite of the violently exploding energy flares that soared up to meet it, it penetrated to within forty miles of the planet's dimly visible surface before it was finally exploded by a direct hit.

In one hour, when the entire scene was still concealed by an impenetrable cloud, they had their first reaction. A transparent, glittering shell, not more than eight feet in diameter, was picked up on the scanners. There was something inside it, but whatever it was refused to resolve into focus.

It came nearer and nearer, and still the thing inside would not show clearly to their straining eyes.

Lesbee III stood on the bridge beside the chair in which his grandfather sat. And the sweat broke out on his brow. When the shell was two hundred yards distant, he said: "Do you think we ought to let it come any nearer?"

The old man's glance was contemptuous. "Our screens are up, aren't they? If it's a bomb, it can't touch us."

Lesbee III was silent. He did not share the old man's confidence that Earth's science was equal to anything that might happen in space. He was prepared to admit that he knew very little about Earth's science, but still—that shell.

"It seems to have stopped, sir." That was Carson, pointedly addressing the aged captain, ignoring the acting captain.

The words relieved Lesbee III, but the first officer's action saddened him. What kind of suicidal impulse made Carson think that the temporary presence of the hundred-year-old retired captain was a good reason for insulting the man who would be commander for thirty years more at least?

He forgot that, for the thing in the shell, whatever it was, was watching them intently. Lesbee III felt a hideous thrill. He said jumpily: "Somebody get us a clear picture of it."

The screen blurred, then cleared but the object in the shell looked as confusing as ever. After a moment longer it moved in an unhuman fashion. Instantly the shell began to approach the spaceship again with a disturbingly steady forward movement. Within seconds, it was less than a hundred yards away, and coming nearer.

"He'll never get through the defenses!" Lesbee III said doubtfully.

He tensely watched the shell. At twenty-five yards it was already through the outer defenses not only of the ship but of Lesbee's mind. He couldn't see it. That was the damnable, mind-destroying part. His eyes kept twisting, as if his brain could not accept the image. The sensation was fantastic. His courage slipped from him like a rotted rag. He made a dive for the stairway and was vaguely surprised to find Carson there ahead of him. He felt the burly Browne crowding his heels.

Lesbee III's final memory of the bridge was of the ancient Captain Lesbee sitting stiffly in the great captain's chair—and the alien shell only a few feet from the outer hull.

In the corridor below, he recovered sufficiently to wave his officers to an elevator. He took them down to the alternative control room. They hastily switched on the viewplates that connected with the bridge. The screen flickered with streamers of light but no picture took form. And a steady roaring sound came from the speakers.

It was a dismaying situation; desperately, Lesbee III said, "What could affect our eyes, twist them? Does anyone know of a phenomenon of the physics of light that has that effect?"

It seemed that a number of subvisual lasers could stimulate the visual centers painfully.

And certain levels of fear within the body could twist the eyes from inside.

Those were the only suggestions.

Lesbee III commanded: "Rig something that will reflect the particular lasers you have in mind." To Dr. Kaspar, he said, "What would stimulate fear?"

"Certain sounds."

"There were none."

"Brain-level waves on the exact band of terror."

"Wel-ll"—doubtfully—"we were certainly put to flight, but I didn't actually feel fear. I felt confusion."

"Some kind of an energy field—I'm speculating wildly!" said the psychologist.

"Use the technical staff!" Lesbee III ordered him. "Figure out some kind of interference for all of those possibilities. On the double, everybody!"

They were still frantically working in the shops, when the viewplate in the alternative control room suddenly cleared. Simultaneously, the roar in the speakers ceased. The first picture that showed was of the bridge itself. Lesbee III could see the old captain still in his chair, but slumped over. There was nothing else visible in his line of sight. Hopefully, Lesbee III tuned to the space scanners. To his relief, he saw that the shell was withdrawing; it was already a quarter of a mile away. It receded rapidly, became a speck against the great, misty planet below.

Lesbee III did not wait for it to vanish entirely, but raced for the elevator—with Browne and Carson close behind. They found his grandfather still alive, talking nonsense to himself and, it soon developed, stone blind.

As they carried him down the steps, and then wheeled him to his room, Lesbee listened intently to his muttering. The words that made sense were about the old man's childhood long ago on Earth.

In the room, Lesbee III grasped the thin, cold hands in his own. "Captain! Captain!"

After he had repeated the one word several times, the other's muttering ceased. "Captain, what happened up there on the bridge?"

The old man started to speak. Lesbee III strained and heard a few words:

". . . we forgot the eccentric orbit of *Canis Major* A with its B. We forgot that B is one of the strange suns of the galaxy . . . so dense, so monstrously dense . . . it said it's from the planet of B. . . . It said, get away! They won't deal with anyone who tried to bomb them. . . . Get away! Get away . . . ! It attached something to the hull . . . pictures, it said . . ."

Lesbee III had leaped away to the intercom. He shouted orders for astronauts to go outside, remove whatever was attached to the hull, take it off in a lifeboat, and when they had examined it and found it harmless, bring it back to the ship.

As he turned back to the captain, Lesbee III felt a shock. The face which had momentarily showed some semblance of sanity had changed again. The eyes were all wrong, twisted, crossed, as if they had tried to look at something that they could not focus on. As he watched, more interested now than disturbed, they continued to twist sightlessly.

Lesbee III tried to get the old man's attention as before by addressing him repeatedly. But this time there was no response. The lined and bearded face retained its abnormal expression.

A doctor had come. Two assistants undressed the long, scrawny body and laid it in the bed. Lesbee III departed.

By the dinner hour, the astronauts were back with a weird but harmless package. It contained a transparent, peculiarly-shaped beaker with a colorless liquid inside. When Lesbee III first saw the object, he saw that there was a picture on the inside of the bottle. Eagerly, he picked it up—intending to bring it closer to his eyes—and the picture changed. Another scene took form inside.

The picture changed with every move. Not once, while he looked at it, did any scene repeat. And in order to see a specific frame for more than a fraction of a second, he finally had to lay it down and sit up close to it. By maneuvering it gently with his fingers every few seconds, he was able at last to view the strange world of the inhabitants of Sirius A-1, who, apparently, had originally come from the mysterious planet of B.

At first there were only scenes: landscapes and oceans. What the liquid in the oceans was, was not obvious; the water was tinted yellow. But the initial scenes showed a turbulent liquid that had the look of being storm tossed.

One scene after another showed a rapid succession of huge waves.

When the frames finally began to show land, the scene was of rugged, mountainous country that was covered with a grayish-yellow growth; a kind of moss, it seemed to the intent Lesbee III. Here and there, the growth piled up into uneven shapes, some of which were small and others of which were extremely tall. Because of the jagged appearance, the growths were beautiful—much as a design in gold and silver is beautiful.

There were other growths, but they were a tiny proportion of the whole: a touch of red, or green, a different type of foliage; that was all. The yellow-gray "moss" and the silver-gold "trees" dominated equally the mountain peaks and plains.

Abruptly, there was a city scene.

Everywhere, in that first look, he saw canals filled with what seemed to be water. Enthralled, Lesbee III remembered motion pictures he had seen of the far-distant Earth city of Venice, Italy. This seemed similar.

Then he saw that the "canals" were on top of the buildings and that there were different levels of them. The high-rise buildings extended for miles like a continuous cliff, uniform in height. Between the two abutments, made up of the front and back of the buildings, flowed two streams of the yellow-tinted "water" . . . in opposite directions.

Each of the three levels of lower-rise buildings also had its two streams. The entire array of buildings periodically crisscrossed with others of their own type, which came in upon them at right angles.

. . . Square on square mile of each, and thousands of canals . . . no streets visible anywhere; simply the solid masses of buildings presenting four roof levels, and every roof with water on it.

In the water were dark shapes—that moved. He couldn't see them.

The picture frames that showed these creatures close up had a light effect that twisted Lesbee III's eyes.

He was amazed, interested, intensely disappointed. "I'll be damned," he said. "They don't want us to see what they look like."

Physicist Plauck, peering over Lesbee's shoulder, said, "On such a huge planet, it follows that the muscles of a life form would require a buoyant liquid to support the body. If their planet of origin is B-1—which is larger—then, like Earth man on Mars, what we're seeing is the intelligent life form of this system in an environment where its motion is actually freer than on its home planet. Yet they still need additional support. It suggests a very dense physical structure, hard to handle."

Lesbee III, whose eyes were beginning to hurt, stood up. "Take this bottle," he said, "and film the pictures inside it. We'll have a general showing for everybody later."

He added, "After you've made the film, see if you can't figure out their method of putting pictures into bottles. They must know a lot more about the physics and chemistry of liquids than we do."

With that, he headed back to his grandfather's room. He found the old man in a coma.

Captain John Lesbee, first commander of the *Hope of Man,* died in the sleep hour that same sidereal day, seventy-seven years, four months, and nine days out from Earth, at the honorable age of one hundred and thirty-one years.

Within six months, no man or woman of his generation remained alive.

It was then that Lesbee III made a major error. He attempted to carry out his purpose of getting rid of a no-longer-needed Atkins.

The death of Lesbee III at the hands of Atkins—who was immediately executed despite his plea of self-defense—created a new crisis aboard the *Hope of Man.*

John Lesbee IV was only ten years old and, though it was urged by Browne that he be made captain at once, First Officer Carson thought otherwise. "It is true," he said sanctimoniously, "that he will be grown up by the time we reach Procyon, but in the meantime we will establish a captain's council to command for him."

In this he was supported by Second Officer Luthers. And several weeks went by before Browne discovered the two wives of Lesbee III were now living with Carson and Luthers.

"You old goats!" he said, at the next meeting of the captain's council. "I demand an immediate election. And if you don't agree right now, I'm going to the scientists, and to the crew."

He stood up, and towered over the smaller men. The older men shrank back, and then Carson tried to draw a blaster from an inside pocket. When he was in a hurry, Browne did not know his own strength. He grabbed the two men, and bumped their heads together. The power of that bump was too much for human bone and flesh, particularly since Browne's rage did not permit him to stop immediately.

The developing limpness of the two bodies in his grasp finally brought him out of his passion. When full realization penetrated, he called the scientists into session, and it was then decided to hold an election.

It required a while to make the people understand what was wanted, but finally an executive council was duly elected by secret ballot. And this council recognized the right of John Lesbee IV to succeed his father as captain, when he reached maturity. In the meantime the council offered the temporary captaincy to Browne, for a term of one year.

By the following year, two of the council members had thought over the situation, and offered themselves as candidates for the captaincy. Browne was reelected.

The former third officer, now Acting Captain Browne, was vaguely annoyed at the opposition that had developed to him.

"Why," he said in a hurt tone, to his eldest son, "they don't know anything about the duties of an officer."

He began to train his two sons in the details of the work. "You might as well know something about it," he said. "Somebody's got to."

For a while his conscience bothered him, and then he began to hear that there was a campaign of vilification being carried on against him. "Things never used to be like this," he complained to the council. "When donkeys like young Kesser and that middle-aged goat Plauck can call you a fool behind your back, there's something wrong. I think maybe next year you fellows had better appoint me captain until Lesbee is twenty-five years old, and end that kind of nonsense. We can't take the chance of some nut who doesn't understand how this ship works, taking control."

Councillor Plauck commented dryly that a knowledge of physics was a handy adjunct to any commander in a space cluttered with dangerous energies such as the cosmic rays. Browne's "recommendation," as it was called, was refused. But he was reappointed to the captaincy for another year.

It was shortly after this that one of the councillors, passing through the hydroponic gardens, saw a familiar face among the workers. He reported to the council, and an emergency meeting was called. Browne was suave. "Why shouldn't young Lesbee limber up his muscles a little? This idea of a separate hierarchy is all wrong. In my opinion, all the young people should work in the gardens for a time every year. I'm going to have that put to a vote. I'll bet the regular garden workers would just love to have you big shots come around and tell them that there are people aboard this ship who are too good to do manual labor."

Later, when he was asked about the progress of young Lesbee in his officer training, Browne shook his head, with due gravity. "Frankly, gentlemen, his progress is poor. I have him come up to the bridge every day after he's through at the gardens. And he just doesn't take any interest. I'm coming to the conclusion, reluctantly, that he just isn't very bright. He just can't learn well."

It was clear to some of the council members at least, that Captain Browne was learning very "well" indeed.

11

John Lesbee IV did not pause in his picking of the ripened fruit. The nearest wall of the hydroponic gardens was two hundred feet away, but his caution was boundless. He listened with a deliberate casualness as the girl spoke to him: "Mother says the sparks started two days ago. So we must be near Procyon."

Lesbee IV said nothing. He accepted the old explanation for the spark phenomenon, that they occurred wherever there were two or more suns to draw huge numbers of high-energy particles from each other's magnetic fields and accelerate them far out into interstellar space.

Although his pretense at leadership was wearing thin, he had "policies," one of which was that he did not discuss technical matters with his followers. He had given the girl her instructions the "night" before. It was now up to her to make a report.

His fingers continued their automatic movements as she

went on: "The others think you should run in this election. Browne is putting his oldest son up for the council. If we can elect you in his place—" She stopped; then: "Remember, you're now twenty-nine years old. And the council still has paid no attention to your rights. You'll have to fight for them."

Lesbee IV made no answer. He felt a weariness at these stupid people who were always urging him to come out into the open. Didn't they realize the danger? And besides, it was important to wait till they had been to Procyon. Then, with Earth as the next destination, the scoundrels who had cheated him out of his rights would begin to think twice.

"If you don't act," said the girl anxiously, "the men are going to take things into their own hands. They're tired—we're all tired—of doing all the hard work, and getting the poorest food. Gourdy says"—she paused—"we'll take the ship."

She sounded awed. And for the first time Lesbee made a dismissing motion that had nothing to do with fruit picking. "Aaaaa!" he said, and brought his hand down, contemptuously. These ignorant fools, he thought. They didn't know what they were talking about.

Take the ship indeed—a bunch of working people, who had never even seen space, except on a screen.

"You'd better hurry!" the girl said. "You'd better hurry and make up your mind—"

The vague reports of the underground resurrection that was developing failed to disturb Captain Browne. "Those dirty beggars," he said to Lieutenant George Browne, his younger son and chief officer of the ship, "haven't enough brains to steal my hat. Besides, just wait until they find out what my plans are when we get into the Procyon system. That'll make them think twice."

The younger Browne said nothing. He considered his father a fool, and it had already struck him that it would be a long, long time before the burly captain would start to decline seriously. At a hundred and four, the commander looked good for another twenty years.

It was a long time to wait for the captaincy. He'd be an old man himself before it happened. The subject was one that he had already discussed with his elder brother, who was due to run for the council at the elections next month.

Perhaps he should also let the underground group become aware of the tenor of his thoughts. A few vague promises—

Procyon A, with six times the luminosity of Sol, swam in the darkness ahead. A yellow-white sun, it loomed larger and larger, brighter and brighter. In the blackness, billions of miles to one side, Procyon B was a pale husk of a sun, clearly visible only in the telescopes.

Surprisingly, Procyon boasted more planets than had the brilliant, the massively bright Sirius. Twenty-five huge worlds revealed themselves in the telescopes. The ship investigated the two, with diameters of twenty-five thousand miles, found both were inhabited, and both had predominantly chlorine atmospheres.

"Those other fellows had good ideas," said Captain Browne, "but they never gave these alien civilizations credit for goodwill. The thing we've got to remember is, not once have the inhabitants of these systems made any attempt to harm us. You may say, what about old Captain Lesbee? Nonsense, I say. He looked at something that wasn't for human eyes, it wrecked his brain, and he died. The important thing is, that thing in the shell that looked at him had the ship completely at its mercy, and it made no effort to do damage.

"So!" The big captain looked around the council room. "Where does that leave us? In the best position we've ever been in. Old man Lesbee didn't dare to force issues at Centaurus because he was dealing with the unknown. At Sirius we got scared and beat it because the unknown showed itself to be absolutely and completely unhuman. But now we know. There seems to be an interstellar civilization here, and it can tell us what we want to know. What do we want to know? Why, which stars have Earth-sized planets with oxygen atmospheres.

"They don't care if we find them. Why should they? Oxygen planets are forever beyond their reach, just as sulfur and chlorine planets are beyond ours.

"All right then, let's tell them what we want to know. How?" He grinned triumphantly at his audience. "Just leave it to me," he said. "Just leave it to me. The first of their ships we can get near will find out."

Actually, it was the fourth ship that found out. The first three ignored the *Hope of Man*. The fourth one came to a full stop in the space of a score of miles. It returned to within a hundred yards of the Earth ship, and remained quiet throughout the whole of the show that Browne put on.

The mechanism he used was simple enough. He rigged a

huge motion-picture screen inside one of the lifeboats, then sent the lifeboat outside. The projector was mounted inside the bridge, and the series of pictures that followed showed the *Hope of Man* leaving Earth, arriving first at Alpha Centauri, then at Sirius and the discovery that the inhabited planets were based on chlorine and sulfur atmospheres respectively. This was shown by the simple method of projecting beside the planets pictures of the atomic structures of chlorine and sulfur. Earth was pictured with oxygen and nitrogen, although it was assumed that these beings would understand that it was the oxygen that made life possible.

Then began the most important phase of the weird showing. A star map was flashed onto the screen. It pictured sixty-odd stars within twenty light-years of Sol. Onto this scene was imposed a triumvirate of atomic structures—chlorine, oxygen, sulfur. The trio was jerked in front of one sun, held for a moment, then moved on to another.

"Let's see," said Browne, "how quickly they catch on that we don't know what kind of atmosphere the planets on those stars have."

They caught on as the camera was moving its three-headed question mark from the sixth to the seventh star. They acted by blotting out the moving trio. Onto the stationary map they imposed a solid rank of atomic structures, one beside each star.

Browne counted four that were shown as having oxygen atmospheres. As he watched, another star map was synchronized with the Earth one. It showed thousands of suns, and beside each one was the revealing atomic symbol that indicated the nature of the atmospheres of the habitable planets.

He saw that the alien ship was moving away; its image on the screen swiftly grew smaller.

"Get the lifeboat in!" Browne commanded. "I guess we'd better get started, too. I think I'll recommend that we go to Alta. That's the nearest."

Later, as he reported to the council, there was an almost fatuous smile on his large face. He was proud of himself. His plan had worked, and so an Earth-born vessel had a film record of scores, perhaps hundreds, of planets that might be colonized by human beings.

The feeling of success suffused him, as he let his gaze move from face to face. He wondered if these councillors were thinking what they should: how right they had been to elect him captain at their annual meetings. Perhaps, they would now see the wisdom of dispensing with elections altogether. The election system was really very dangerous and was against the rules by which vessels of the armed forces were administered. The matter should be settled so that there would be no confusion if anything ever happened to him.

It wasn't—he told himself—that he felt old. But he computed that it would take thirty years to reach Alta, and it might well be that he would not survive another three decades. For strictly emotional reasons, he wanted the right to name his successor. He desired the captaincy to go to his second son.

As he had that thought, his moving gaze touched the doorknob across the room. He saw it turn; he had a peculiar, lightning intuition—

And he snatched his blaster . . .

The promptness of his reaction protected the ship from the hands of the rebels but did not save his own life. Later, when the younger Browne led a group of armed technicians and scientists to the aid of the council, they found all but one member dead and that one seriously injured. Captain Browne and his eldest son were both victims of the rebellion. Plauck and Kesser were hardly recognizable, but they had apparently had time to draw their weapons and to fire at the rebel group led by Gourdy. Lesbee IV, it developed, had refused to participate.

Of the more than twenty young men who had aided Gourdy, seventeen were dead. A trail of blood led along the corridor, first to two severely wounded men, and then to a storeroom where Gourdy had barricaded himself.

Since he would not surrender, they used their greater knowledge of the ship against him. A needle gun was silently pushed through one wall from a secret passageway. He never knew what killed him.

The new Captain Browne, being over seventy years old himself, thoughtfully had the injured councillor carried to the captain's bed. Somewhere, late in the sleep period, the acting captain considered the problem presented by one living survivor of a group of electors and he shook his head, finally and with decision.

"If he lives," he thought "the whole election system may be rehabilitated and that is absolutely ridiculous."

Presently, he called his son on the intercom. The two

men—the son was forty-five years of age at this time—agreed that the father's judgment was correct. At the older man's suggestion, the younger Browne returned to his own room.

But he was not surprised to hear his father report at the end of the sleep period that the wounded councillor was dead.

And that there was no one left aboard entitled to demand an election.

12

One hundred and nine years after leaving Earth, the spaceship, *Hope of Man*, went into orbit around Alta III, the only inhabited and habitable planet they had found in the system.

The following "morning," Captain Browne informed the shipload of fourth- and fifth-generation colonists that a manned lifeboat would be sent to the planet's surface.

"Every member of the crew must consider himself expendable," he said earnestly. "This is the day that our great-grandparents, our forefathers, who boldly set out for the new space frontier so long ago, looked forward to with unfaltering courage. We must not fail them."

He concluded his announcement over the speaker system of the big ship by saying that the names of the crew members of the lifeboat would be given out within the hour, "And I know that every real man aboard will want to see his name there."

John Lesbee, the fifth of his line aboard, had a sinking sensation as he heard those words—and he was not mistaken in his sudden premonition.

Even as he tried to decide if he should give the signal for a desperate act of rebellion, Captain Browne made the expected announcement.

The commander said, "And I know you will all join him in his moment of pride and courage when I tell you that John

Lesbee will lead the crew that carries the hopes of man in this remote area of space. And now the others—"

He thereupon named seven of the nine persons with whom Lesbee had been conspiring to seize control of the ship.

Since the lifeboat would only hold eight persons, Lesbee recognized that Browne was dispatching as many of his enemies as he could. He listened with developing dismay, as the commander ordered all persons on the ship to come to the recreation room. "Here I request that the crew of the lifeboat join me and the other officers. Their instructions are to surrender themselves to any craft which seeks to intercept them. Their scanners will relay all observed events to us here, and enable us to determine the level of scientific attainment of the dominant race on the planet below."

Lesbee hurried to his room on the technicians' deck, hoping that perhaps Tellier or Cantlin would seek him out there. He felt himself in need of a council of war, however brief. He waited five minutes, but not one member of the conspiratorial group showed.

Nonetheless, he had time to grow calm. Peculiarly, it was the smell of the ship that soothed him most. From the earliest days of his life, the odor of ozone and the scent of metal at high temperature had been perpetual companions. At the moment, with the ship in orbit, there was a letting up of stress. The smell was of old energies rather than new. But the effect was similar.

He sat in the chair he used for reading, eyes closed, breathing in that complex of odors, product of so many titanic energies. He felt the fear leave his mind and body. He grew brave again, and strong.

Lesbee recognized that his plan to seize power had involved risks. Worse, no one would question Browne's choice of him as the leader of the mission. "I am," thought Lesbee, "probably the most highly trained technician ever to be on this ship." Browne III had taken him when he was ten, and started him on the long grind of learning that led him to master, one after the other, the skills of the various technical departments. And Browne IV had continued his training.

He was taught how to repair control systems. He gradually came to understand the interrelated cybernetic functions. Long ago, the colossal cobweb of electronic circuitry behind the many panels had become almost an extension of his own nervous system.

He never did find time to learn the basic theory of the ship's main drive. This information was contained in a course of study to which Browne had provided access, and so a little knowledge had come through to him and stayed with him. But in these advanced realms, he actually knew less than his father.

His father had made numerous attempts to pass his knowledge on to his son. But it was as hard to teach complexities to a tired and sleepy boy as it had been for the older man to learn those complexities himself under similar circumstances. Lesbee even felt slightly relieved when his parent died. It took the pressure off him. Since then, however, he had come to realize that the Browne family, by forcing a lesser skill on the descendant of the original commander of the ship, had won their greatest victory.

As he finally headed for the recreation room, Lesbee found himself wondering: Had the Brownes trained him with the intention of preparing him for such a mission as this?

His eyes widened. If that were true, then his own conspiracy was merely an excuse. The decision to kill him might actually have been made more than a decade ago, and light-years away. . . .

As the lifeboat rocketed toward Alta III, Lesbee and Tellier sat in the twin control chairs and watched on the forward screen the vast, misty atmosphere of the planet. Dr. Tellier had never understood why spaceships could not attain even a quarter of the speed of light. His records showed that he had hoped to reach velocities greater than light, but his death had occurred too soon for him to train his son to carry on after him. No one since had had the necessary knowledge to continue his work.

It was vaguely believed by the scientists who succeeded Dr. Tellier that the ship had run into one of the paradoxes implicit in the Lorentz-Fitzgerald Contraction Theory.

Whatever the explanation, it was never solved.

Watching Tellier, Lesbee wondered if his companion and best friend felt as empty inside as he did. Incredibly, this was the first time he—or anyone—had been outside the big ship. "We're actually heading down," he thought, "to one of those great masses of land and water, a planet."

As he watched, fascinated, the massive ball grew visibly bigger.

They came in at a slant, a long, swift, angling approach, ready to jet away if any of the natural radiation belts proved too much for their defense systems. But as each stage of radiation registered in turn, the dials showed that the lifeboat machinery made the proper responses automatically.

The silence was shattered suddenly by an alarm bell.

Simultaneously, one of the screens focused on a point of rapidly moving light far below. The light darted toward them.

A missile!

Lesbee caught his breath.

But the shining point of light veered off, turned completely around, took up position several miles away, and began to fall with them.

His first thought was: "They'll never let us land," and he experienced intense disappointment.

Another signal sounded from the control board.

"They're probing us," said Tellier, tensely.

An instant after the words were uttered, the lifeboat seemed to shudder and to stiffen under them. It was the unmistakable feel of a tractor beam, probing from the other craft. Its field clutched the lifeboat, drew it, held it.

The science of the Alta III inhabitants was already proving itself formidable.

Underneath him, the lifeboat continued its movement.

The entire crew gathered around and watched as the point of brightness came closer, resolved into an object, which rapidly grew larger. It loomed up close, bigger than they.

There was a metallic bump. The lifeboat shuddered from stem to stern.

Even before the vibrations ceased, Tellier said, "Notice they put our airlock against theirs."

Behind Lesbee, his companions began that peculiar joking of the threatened. It was a coarse comedy, but suddenly it had enough actual humor to break through his fear. Involuntarily, he found himself laughing.

Then, momentarily free of anxiety, aware that Browne was watching and that there was no escape, he said, "Open the airlock! Let the aliens capture us as ordered."

13

A few minutes after the outer airlock was opened, the airlock of the alien ship also folded back. Rubberized devices rolled out and contacted the Earth lifeboat, sealing off both entrances from the vacuum of space.

Air hissed into the interlocking passageway between the two crafts. In the alien craft's lock, an inner door opened.

Again Lesbee held his breath.

There was a movement in the passageway. A creature ambled into view. The being came forward with complete assurance, and pounded on the hull with something he held at the end of one of his four leathery arms.

The creature had four legs and four arms, and a long, thin body held straight up. It had almost no neck, yet the many skin folds between the head and the body indicated great flexibility was possible.

Even as Lesbee noted the details of its appearance, the being turned its head slightly, and its two large expressionless eyes gazed straight at the hidden wall scanner that was photographing the scene, and therefore straight into Lesbee's eyes.

Lesbee blinked at the creature, then tore his gaze away, swallowed hard, and nodded at Tellier. "Open up!" he commanded.

The moment the inner door of the Earth lifeboat opened, six more of the four-legged beings appeared, one after another, in the passageway, and walked forward in the same confident way as had the first.

All seven creatures entered the open door of the lifeboat.

As they entered, their thoughts came instantly into Lesbee's mind. . . .

As Dzing and his boarding party trotted from the small Karn ship through the connecting airlock, his chief officer thought a message to him.

"Air pressure and oxygen content are within a tiny per-

52

centage of what exists at ground level on Karn. They can certainly live on our planet."

Dzing moved forward into the Earth ship, and realized that he was in the craft's control chamber. Then, for the first time, he saw the men. He and his crew ceased their forward motion, and the two groups of beings—the human and the Karn—gazed at each other.

The appearance of the two-legged beings did not surprise Dzing. Pulse viewers had, earlier, penetrated the metal walls of the lifeboat and had accurately photographed the shapes and dimensions of those aboard.

His first instruction to his crew was designed to test whether the strangers were, in fact, surrendering. He commanded: "Convey to the prisoners that we require them, as a precaution, to remove their clothing."

. . . Until that direction was given, Lesbee was still uncertain as to whether or not these beings could receive human thoughts as he was receiving theirs. From the first moment, the aliens had conducted their mental conversations *as if* they were unaware of the thoughts of the human beings. Now as he watched, the Karn came forward. One tugged suggestively at his clothing. And there was no doubt.

The mental telepathy was a one-way flow only—from the Karn to the humans.

He was already savoring the implications of that as he hastily undressed. . . . It was absolutely vital that Browne should not find out about this.

Lesbee removed all his clothes; then, before putting them down, took out his notebook and pen. Standing there naked, he wrote hurriedly:

"Don't let on that we can read the minds of these beings."

He handed the notebook around, and he felt easier as each of the men read it, and nodded at him silently.

Dzing communicated telepathically with someone on the ground. "These strangers," he reported, "clearly acted under command to surrender. The problem is, how can we now let them overcome us, without arousing their suspicion that this is what we want them to do?"

Lesbee did not receive the answer directly. But he picked it up from Dzing's mind: "Start tearing the lifeboat apart. See if that brings a reaction."

The members of the Karn boarding party went to work at once. Off came the control panels. The floor plates were melted and ripped up. Soon instruments, wiring, controls were exposed for examination.

Browne must have watched the destruction; for now, before the Karn could start wrecking the automatic machinery, his voice commanded:

"Watch out, you men! I'm going to shut your airlock and cause your boat to make a sharp right turn in exactly twenty seconds."

For Lesbee and Tellier, that simply meant sitting down in their chairs and turning them so that the acceleration pressure would press them against the backs. The other men sank to the ripped-up floor, and braced themselves.

Underneath Dzing, the ship swerved. The turn began slowly, but he permitted it to propel him over to one wall of the control room. There, he grabbed with his numerous hands at some handholds that had suddenly moved out from the smooth metal. By the time the turn grew sharper, he had his four short legs braced, and he took the rest of the wide swing around with every part of his long, sleek body taut. His companions did the same. They all pretended to be affected by inertia.

Presently, the awful pressure eased up, and he was able to estimate that their new direction was almost at right angles to what it had been.

He had reported what was happening while it was going on. Now, the answer came: "Keep on destroying. See what they do, and be prepared to succumb to anything that looks like a lethal attack."

Lesbee wrote quickly in his notebook: "Our method of capturing them doesn't have to be subtle. They'll make it easy for us—so we can't lose."

Lesbee waited tensely as the notebook was passed around. It was still hard for him to believe that no one else had noticed what he had about this boarding party.

Tellier added a note of his own: "It's obvious now that these beings were also instructed to consider themselves expendable."

And that settled it for Lesbee. The others hadn't noticed what he had. He sighed with relief at the false analysis, for it gave him that most perfect of all advantages: that which derived from his special education.

Apparently, he alone knew enough to have analyzed what these creatures were.

The proof was in the immense clarity of their thoughts. Long ago, on earth, it had been established that man had a faltering telepathic ability, which could be utilized consistently only by electronic amplification *outside* his brain. The amount of energy needed for the step-up process was enough to burn out brain nerves if applied directly.

Since the Karn were utilizing it directly, they couldn't be living beings.

Therefore, Dzing and his fellows were an advanced robot type.

The true inhabitants of Alta III were not risking their own skins at all.

Far more important to Lesbee, he could see how he might use these marvelous mechanisms to defeat Browne, take over the *Hope of Man,* and start the long journey back to Earth.

14

He had been watching the Karn at their work of destruction, while he had these thoughts. Now, he said aloud: "Hainker, Graves."

"Yes?" The two men spoke together.

"In a few moments I'm going to ask Captain Browne to turn the ship again. When he does, use our specimen gas guns!"

The men grinned with relief. "Consider it done," said Hainker.

Lesbee ordered the other four crewmen to be ready to use the specimen-holding devices at top speed. To Tellier he said, "You take charge if anything happens to me."

Then he wrote one more message in the notebook: "These beings will probably continue their mental intercommunication after they are apparently rendered unconscious. Pay no attention, and do not comment on it in any way."

He felt a lot better when that statement also had been read by the others, and the notebook was once more in his possession. Quickly, he spoke to the screen:

"Captain Browne! Make another turn, just enough to pin them."

And so they captured Dzing and his crew.

As he had expected, the Karn continued their telepathic conversation. Dzing reported to his ground contact: "I think we did that rather well."

There must have been an answering message from below, because he went on, "Yes, Commander. We are now prisoners as per your instructions, and shall await events. . . . The imprisoning method? Each of us is pinned down by a machine that has been placed astride us, with the main section adjusted to the contours of our bodies. A series of rigid metal appendages fasten our arms and legs. All these devices are electronically controlled, and we can, of course, escape at any time. Naturally such action is for later. . . ."

Lesbee was chilled by the analysis; but for expendables there was no turning back.

He ordered his men: "Get dressed. Then start repairing the ship. Put all the floor plates back, except the section at G-8. They removed some of the instruments, and I'd better make sure myself that it all goes back all right."

When he had dressed, he reset the course of the lifeboat, and called Browne. The screen lit up after a moment, and there, staring back at him, was the unhappy countenance of the forty-year-old officer.

Browne said glumly: "I want to congratulate you and your crew on your accomplishments. It would seem that we have a small scientific superiority over this race, and that we can attempt a landing."

Since there would never be a landing on Alta III, Lesbee simply waited without comment, as Browne seemed lost in thought.

The officer stirred finally. He still seemed uncertain. "Mr. Lesbee," he said, "as you must understand, this is an extremely dangerous situation for me—and—" he added hastily, "—for this entire expedition."

What struck Lesbee, as he heard those words, was that Browne was not going to let him back on the ship. But he had to get aboard to accomplish his own purpose. He thought: "I'll have to bring this whole conspiracy out into the open, and apparently make a compromise offer."

He drew a deep breath, gazed straight into the eyes of Browne's image on the screen, and said, with the complete courage of a man for whom there is no turning back: "It seems to me, sir, that we have two alternatives. We can resolve all these personal problems either through a democratic election or by a joint captaincy, you being one of the captains and I being the other."

To any other person who might have been listening, the remark must have seemed a complete non sequitur. Browne, however, understood its relevance. He said with a sneer, "So you've come out in the open. Well, let me tell you, Mr. Lesbee, there was never any talk of elections when the Lesbees were in power. And for a very good reason. A spaceship requires a technical aristocracy to command it. As for a joint captaincy, it wouldn't work."

Lesbee urged his lie: "If we're going to stay here, we'll need at least two people of equal authority—one on the ground, one on the ship."

"I couldn't trust you on the ship!" said Browne flatly.

"Then you be on the ship," Lesbee proposed. "All such practical details can be arranged."

The older man must have been almost beside himself with the intensity of his own feelings on this subject. He flashed, "Your family has been out of power for over fifty years! How can you still feel that you have any rights?"

Lesbee countered, "How come you know what I'm talking about?"

Browne said, a grinding rage in his tone, "The concept of inherited power was introduced by the first Lesbee. It was never planned."

"But here you are," said Lesbee, "yourself a beneficiary of inherited power."

Browne said, from between clenched teeth, "It's absolutely ridiculous that the Earth government which was in power when the ship left—and every member of which has long been dead—should appoint somebody to a command position . . . and that now his descendant thinks that command post should be his, and his family's, for all time!"

Lesbee was silent, startled by the dark emotions he had uncovered in the man. He felt even more justified, if that were possible, and advanced his next suggestion without a qualm.

"Captain, this is a crisis. We should postpone our private struggle. Why don't we bring one of these prisoners aboard so that we can question him by use of the films, or play acting? Later, we can discuss your situation and mine."

He saw from the look on Browne's face that the reasonableness of the suggestion, *and its potentialities,* were penetrating.

Browne said quickly, "Only you come aboard—and with one prisoner. No one else!"

Lesbee felt a dizzying thrill as the man responded to his bait. He thought: "It's like an exercise in logic. He'll try to murder me as soon as he gets me alone and is satisfied that he can attack without danger to himself. But that very scheme is what will get me aboard, and I've got to get on the ship to carry out *my* plan."

Browne was frowning. He said in a concerned tone: "Mr. Lesbee, can you think of any reason why we should not bring one of these beings aboard?"

Lesbee shook his head. "No reason, sir," he lied.

Browne seemed to come to a decision. "Very well. I'll see you shortly, and we can then discuss additional details."

Lesbee dared not say another word. He nodded, and broke the connection, shuddering, disturbed, uneasy.

"But," he thought, "what else can we do?"

He turned his attention to the part of the floor left open for him. Quickly he bent down and studied the codes on each of the programming units, as if he were seeking exactly the right ones that had previously been in those slots.

He found the series he wanted: an intricate system of cross-connected units that had originally been designed to program a remote-control landing system, an advanced Waldo mechanism capable of landing the craft on a planet and taking off again, all directed on the pulse level of human thought.

He slid each unit of the series into its sequential position and locked it in.

Then, that important task completed, he picked up the remote-control attachment for the series and casually put it in his pocket.

He returned to the control board and spent several minutes examining the wiring and comparing it with a wall chart. A number of wires had been torn loose. These he now reconnected, and at the same time he managed with a twist of his pliers to short-circuit a key relay of the remote-control pilot.

Lesbee replaced the panel itself loosely. There was no time to connect it properly. And, since he would easily justify his next move, he pulled a cage out of the storeroom. Into this he hoisted Dzing, manacles and all.

Before lowering the lid, he rigged into the cage a simple resistance network that would prevent the Karn from broadcasting on the human-thought level. The device was simple merely in that it was not selective. It had an on-off switch which triggered, or stopped, energy flow in the metal walls on the thought level.

When the device was installed, Lesbee slipped the tiny remote control for it into his other pocket. He did not activate the control. Not yet.

From the cage, Dzing telepathed: "It is significant that these beings have selected me for this special attention. We might conclude that it is a matter of mathematical accident, or else that they are very observant and so noticed that I was the one who directed activities. Whatever the reason, it would be foolish to turn back now."

A bell began to ring. As Lesbee watched, a spot of light appeared high on one of the screens. It moved rapidly toward some crossed lines in the exact center of the screen. Inexorably, then, the *Hope of Man*, as represented by the light, and the lifeboat moved toward their fateful rendezvous.

15

Browne's instructions were: "Come to the alternate control room."

Lesbee guided his powered dolly with the cage on it, out of the big ship's airlock B—and saw that the man in the control room of the lock was Second Officer Selwyn. Heavy brass for such a routine task. Selwyn waved at him with a twisted smile, as Lesbee wheeled his cargo along the silent corridor.

He saw no one else on his route. Other personnel had evidently been cleared from this part of the vessel. A little later, grim and determined, he set the cage down in the center of the auxiliary control room and anchored it magnetically to the floor.

Browne climbed out of his control chair and stepped down from the rubber-sheathed dais to the same level as Lesbee. He came forward, smiling, his hand held out. He was a big man, as all the Brownes had been, bigger by a head than Lesbee, and good-looking in a clean-cut way. The two men were alone.

"I'm glad you were so frank," he said. "I doubt if I could have spoken so bluntly to you, without your initiative as an example."

But as they shook hands, Lesbee was wary and suspicious, thinking: "He's trying to recover from the insanity of his reaction. I really blew him wide open."

Browne continued in the same hearty tone, "I've made up my mind. An election is out of the question. The ship is swarming with untrained dissident groups, most of which simply want to go back to Earth."

Lesbee, who had the same desire, was discreetly silent.

Browne said, "You'll be ground captain. I'll be ship captain. Why don't we sit down right now and work out a communiqué on which we can agree and that I can read over the speakers to everyone aboard?"

As Lesbee seated himself in the chair beside Browne, he was thinking: "What can be gained from publicly naming me ground captain?"

He concluded finally, cynically, that the older man could gain the confidence of John Lesbee—lull him, lead him on, delude him, destroy him.

Surreptitiously, Lesbee examined the room. The auxiliary control room was a large square chamber adjoining the massive central engines. Its control board was a duplicate of the one on the bridge located at the top of the ship. The great vessel could be guided equally from either board, except that pre-emptive power was on the bridge. The officer of the watch was given the right to make merit decisions in an emergency.

Lesbee made a quick mental calculation, and deduced that it was First Officer Miller's watch on the bridge. Miller was a stanch supporter of Browne. The man was probably watching them on one of the screens, ready to come to the aid of Browne at a moment's notice.

A few minutes later, Lesbee listened thoughtfully as Browne read their joint communiqué over the intercom, designating him as ground captain. He found himself a little amazed, and considerably dismayed, at the absolute confidence the older man must feel about his own power and position on the ship. It was a big step, naming his chief rival to so high a rank.

Browne's next act was equally surprising. While they were still on the viewers, Browne reached over, clapped Lesbee affectionately on the shoulders and said to the watching audience:

"As you all know, John is the only direct descendant of the original captain. No one knows exactly what happened half a hundred years ago when my grandfather first took command. But I remember the old man always felt that only he understood how things should be. I doubt if he had any confidence in *any* young whippersnapper over whom he did not have complete control. I often felt that my father was the victim rather than the beneficiary of my grandfather's temper and feelings of superiority."

Browne smiled engagingly. "Anyway, good people, though we can't unbreak the eggs that were broken then, we can certainly start healing the wounds, without"—his tone was suddenly firm—"negating the fact that my own training and experience make me the proper commander of the ship itself."

He broke off. "Captain Lesbee and I shall now jointly attempt to communicate with the captured intelligent life form from the planet below. You may watch, though we reserve the right to cut you off for good reason." He turned to Lesbee. "What do you think we should do first, John?"

Lesbee was in a dilemma. The first large doubt had come to him, the possibility that perhaps the other was sincere. The possibility was especially disturbing because in a few moments a part of his own plan would be revealed.

He sighed, and realized that there was no turning back at this stage. He thought: "We'll have to bring the entire madness out into the open, and only then can we begin to consider agreement as real."

Aloud, he said in a steady voice, "Why not bring the prisoner out where we can see him?"

As the tractor beam lifted Dzing out of the cage, and thus

away from the energies that had suppressed his thought waves, the Karn telepathed to his contact on Alta III:

"Have been held in a confined space, the metal of which was energized against communication. I shall now attempt to perceive and evaluate the condition and performance of this ship—"

At that point, Browne reached over and clicked off the speaker system. Having shut off the audience, he turned accusingly to Lesbee, and said, "Explain your failure to inform me that these beings communicated by telepathy."

The tone of his voice was threatening. There was a glint of anger in his eyes.

It was the moment of discovery.

Lesbee hesitated, and then simply pointed out how precarious their relationship had been. He finished frankly, "I thought by keeping it a secret I might be able to stay alive a little longer, which was certainly not what you intended when you sent me out as an expendable."

Browne snapped, "But how did you hope to utilize—?" He stopped. "Never mind," he muttered.

Dzing was telepathing again:

"In many ways this ship is very advanced. All automatic systems are well designed and largely self-repairing. There is high-level energy-screen equipment and they can generate a tractor beam to match any we can produce with mobile units. But the atomic-energy drive is most inefficient. The resonating-field coils which control particle acceleration are improperly balanced, as if the basic principle were not fully understood. Instead of being accelerated to near light-speed, the particles are ejected at relatively low velocities where their mass has hardly increased at all. There is not enough mass in the entire ship to have maintained the reactive mode more than a fraction of the distance from the nearest planetary system. Let me furnish you with the data that I am perceiving, for the large computers to interpret . . ."

Lesbee said in alarm, "Quick, sir, drop him back while we figure out what he's talking about!"

Browne did so—as Dzing telepathed: "My analysis is correct! Then these beings are completely at our mercy."

His thought was cut off abruptly, as he was lowered into the cage with its barrier energy.

Browne was turning on the speaker system. He said into it: "Sorry I had to tune you good people out. You'll be interested to know that we managed to read the thought pulses of the prisoner and have intercepted his calls to someone on the planet below. This gives us an advantage." He turned to Lesbee. "Don't you agree, Captain?"

Browne visibly showed no anxiety, whereas Dzing's final statement had flabbergasted Lesbee. ". . . *completely at our mercy . . .*" surely meant exactly that. He was staggered that Browne could have missed the momentous meaning.

Browne addressed him enthusiastically: "I'm excited by this telepathy. It's a marvelous shortcut to communication, if we could build up our own thought pulses. Maybe we could use the principle of the remote-control landing device which, as you know, can project human thoughts on a power-output level comparable to a radio-frequency transmitter."

What interested Lesbee in the suggestion was that he had in his pocket a three-stage remote control for precisely such electronically amplified thought pulses. Unfortunately, the control was for the lifeboat. It probably would be advisable to tune the control to the ship also. It was a problem he had thought of earlier, and now Browne had opened the way for an easy solution.

He held his voice steady as he said, "Captain, let me program those landing analogs while you prepare the film-communication project. That way we can be ready for him, no matter what."

Browne seemed to be completely trusting, for he agreed at once. A film projector was mounted, at Browne's direction, on solid connections at one end of the room. The projectionist and Third Officer Mindel—who had come in with him—strapped themselves into adjoining chairs attached to the projector.

While this was going on, Lesbee called various technical personnel. Only one technician protested. "But, John,' he said, "that way we have a dual control—with the lifeboat control having pre-emption over the ship. It's against all principles of flight guidance to subordinate steady state mechanisms to gadgets. I—it's unusual."

It was unusual. But he was fighting for his life. And it was the lifeboat control that was in his pocket where he could reach it quickly; and so he said adamantly, "Do you want to talk to Captain Browne? Do you want his O.K.?"

"No, no." The technician's doubts seemed to subside. "I

heard you being named joint captain. You're the boss. It shall be done."

Lesbee put down the closed-circuit phone into which he had been talking, and turned. It was then he saw that the film was ready to roll, and that Browne had his fingers on the controls of the tractor beam. The older man stared at him questioningly.

"Shall I go ahead?" he asked.

At this penultimate moment, Lesbee had a qualm.

Almost immediately he realized that the only alternative to what Browne planned was that he reveal his own secret knowledge.

He hesitated, torn by doubts. Then: "Will you turn that off?" He indicated the intercom.

Browne said to the audience, "We'll bring you in again in a minute, good people." He broke the connection and gazed questioningly at Lesbee.

Whereupon Lesbee said in a low voice, "Captain, I should inform you that I brought the Karn aboard in the hope of using him against you."

"Well, that is a frank and open admission," the officer said softly.

"I mention this," said Lesbee, "because if you had similar ulterior motives, we should clear the air completely before proceeding with the attempt at communication."

A blossom of color spread from Browne's neck over his face. At last he said slowly, "I don't know how I can convince you, but I had no schemes."

Lesbee gazed at Browne's open countenance, and suddenly he realized that the officer was sincere. Browne had accepted the compromise. The solution of a joint captaincy was agreeable to him.

Sitting there, Lesbee experienced a mixture of joy and doubt. He could not wholly overcome his fear of Browne's motives. On the other hand, it did seem as if communication worked. You could tell your truth and get a hearing—if it made sense.

It seemed to him that he had to believe that his truth made sense. He was offering Browne peace aboard the ship. Peace at a price, of course; but still peace. And in this severe emergency Browne recognized the entire validity of the solution.

So it was now evident to Lesbee.

Without further hesitation he told Browne that the creatures who had boarded the lifeboat were robots—not alive at all.

Browne was nodding thoughtfully. Finally he said: "But I don't see how this could be utilized to take over the ship."

Lesbee explained that this robot had a built-in self-destruct system, designed in such a way that, when it was activated, it could be pointed so that it would also destroy anything in the path of the blast.

"That," said Lesbee, "is why I had him on his back when I-brought him in here. I could have had him tilted and pointing at you. Naturally, I made sure that this did not happen until you had indicated what you intended to do. One of my precautions would enable us to catch this creature's thoughts without—"

As he was speaking, he slipped his hand into his pocket, intending to show the older man the tiny remote control by which—when it was off—they would be able to read Dzing's thoughts without removing him from the cage.

He stopped short in his explanation because an ugly expression had come suddenly into Browne's face.

The big man glanced at Third Officer Mindel. "Well, Dan," he said, "do you think that's it?"

Lesbee noticed with shock that Mindel was wearing a sound-amplifying device in one ear. He must have overheard every word that Browne and he had spoken to each other.

Mindel nodded. "Yes, Captain," he said. "I very definitely think he has now told us what we wanted to find out."

Lesbee grew aware that Browne had released himself from his safety belt and was stepping away from his seat. The officer turned and, standing very straight, said in a formal tone:

"Technician Lesbee, we have heard your admission of gross dereliction of duty, conspiracy to overthrow the lawful government of this ship, scheme to utilize alien creatures to destroy human beings, and confession of other unspeakable crimes. In this extremely dangerous situation, summary execution without formal trial is justified. I therefore sentence you to death and order Third Officer Mindel to—"

He faltered, and came to a stop.

16

Two things had been happening as he talked. Lesbee squeezed the "off" switch of the cage control, an entirely automatic gesture, convulsive, a spasmodic movement, result of his dismay. It was a mindless action. So far as he knew consciously, freeing Dzing's thoughts had no useful possibility for him. His only real hope—as he realized almost immediately—was to get his other hand into his remaining coat pocket and with it manipulate the remote-control landing device, the secret of which he had so naïvely revealed to Browne.

The second thing that happened was that Dzing, released from mental control, telepathed:

"Free again—and this time of course permanently! I have just now activated by remote control the relays that will in a few moments start the engines of this ship, and I have naturally reset the mechanism for controlling the rate of acceleration—"

The robot's thoughts must have impinged progressively on Browne, for it was at that point that the officer paused uncertainly.

Dzing continued: "As I have rectified the field-control system, the atomic drive will now be able to achieve velocities close to that of light. I have also synchronized the artificial gravity so that there will be a considerable gap between that and the acceleration. They have neglected to take any real precautions against capture by this means—"

Lesbee reached over, tripped on the speaker system, and yelled into the microphone: "All stations prepare for emergency acceleration! Grab anything!"

To Browne, he shouted: "Get to your seat—*quick!*"

His actions and words were automatic responses to danger. Only after he had spoken did it occur to him that he had no interest in the survival of Captain Browne. And that, in fact, the only reason the man was in danger was because he had

66

stepped away from his safety belt so that Mindel's blaster would kill Lesbee without damaging Browne.

Browne evidently understood his danger. He started toward the control chair from which he had released himself moments before. His reaching hands were still a foot or more from it when the impact of acceleration stopped him instantly and flung him backward to the floor. Still going back, he pressed the palms of his hands and his rubber shoes hard against the floor. That probably saved him from a head injury, for his tremendous effort brought him to a sitting position. And so he slid into the rear wall with his back. It was cushioned to protect human beings; it reacted like rubber, bouncing him several times.

Pinned there by several g's of the continuing acceleration, he managed a strangled yell. "Lesbee, put a tractor beam on me. Save me. I'll make it up to you."

The man's wild appeal brought momentary wonder to Lesbee. There was of course nothing he could do. He also was pinned in. But he was amazed that Browne hoped for mercy after what had happened.

The thought and the emotion yielded to the reality that the acceleration was now constant at a bone-breaking intensity. Lesbee became acutely aware of his own awkward position.

He had turned around to speak to Browne, and so he was facing in the wrong direction when the forward drive of the ship hit him. The safety belt and the pit of his stomach had taken the blow. Now, he hung in his belt, doubled up, still in his seat but like a man whose hands and feet were manacled together in front of him. He had the peculiar feeling that his insides would simply flow out of him if there were an opening anywhere in his body. His eyes bulged. The sensation was hideous.

. . . He must swing the chair around so that its back would bear the colossal pressure of acceleration.

He was about to make his first tense effort in that direction, when the lid of the cage lifted and the head of Dzing appeared over its rim. . . . The robot's thoughts had been coming steadily during these momentous seconds.

". . . Well, that was simple enough," the Karn reported. "I have the acceleration gap set at four of their gravities, enough to hold these two-legged beings but not kill them. How long will the boarding party be?" There was a pause and evidently an answer from below, for Dzing said mentally: "That should give me time to investigate the engine room directly. There's some kind of control confusion, which operates on such a tiny level that I'm not programmed to deal with it by remote energies—"

As it made these comments, the creature climbed out of its cage and—without any visible effect from the acceleration—walked to the door and disappeared into the corridor beyond. For a few moments longer, Lesbee was aware that it was continuing its description and discussion. But swiftly, the thought waves grew dim and then faded altogether.

Lesbee became conscious that Browne had also watched Dzing's departure. The two men glared at each other, and then Browne attempted to speak. It was awful to watch him; the acceleration pulled his lips and his mouth muscles, and what came through was a strangled sound. Lesbee made out a few of the words:

". . . Your mad action. . . . We'll be captured . . . destroyed—"

Lesbee thought, "I'll be damned. He's blaming me for our predicament."

He felt a twinge of guilt, but it was momentary. The question of where cause began in a human disaster, when everyone was being human, was not as simple as Browne seemed to believe. . . . Since when, for instance, did a Browne have the right to name a Lesbee as expendable . . . ?

Lesbee did not give voice to these thoughts. He was trying to draw his right arm from its straight-out position in front of him. By bending his elbow, he found movement was not impossible. Cautiously, he forced the arm backward, and with his fingers—and with nearly all his strength—grasped the seat of the control chair . . . fumbled along it to the push-button controls of the chair.

Reached them! Poised his finger on the one that would swing the chair around to face the board—

There he stopped. His mind was beginning to work again. And, though it was like speaking with a cake of soap in his mouth, he gulped at Browne: "How much fuel . . . in engine?"

Impossible to tell from the stunned expression on Browne's face if the question produced a cunning reaction. The commander's muffled answer was: "Many hours!"

Lesbee experienced instant disappointment. For that moment, for that brief moment, he had hopefully recalled the continual talk of fuel shortage. There had even been rumors that during the period of slowing down for Alta there had been times when the engine had only an hour or so of fuel. In fact, he himself had several times been asked to torch-cut metals from hidden parts of the ship. And this he had done, and had taken the product of his effort to the engine room, in the understanding that the drive was ravenous; that the stuff would be used immediately.

If that were so, then where did the present relative plenty come from?

Ruefully, Lesbee realized that the colonists had probably been subjected to a propaganda harassment. There *was*, of course, a fuel shortage. But Browne had exaggerated its immediacy to the point where he had been able to order Lesbee out as an expendable, and no one had said a word.

But regrettably now, he believed Browne. There was fuel in the engines. . . . His brief hope that the available fuel would burn up and release them—was shattered. . . . They'd have to escape from the acceleration pressure some other way. . . . The only method he had was extremely dangerous. Meanwhile, other actions—

Lesbee pressed the button on the side of the control chair.

The chair, power driven, whirled around; the movement did bobbling things to his internal organs, and his legs and arms flip-flopped, were swung about, and forced back. With a thud, he landed breathless against the long, cushioned back of the chair, dizzy but safe and, after a long moment, ready for his next move.

Tensing his arm muscles for the awkward effort, Lesbee forced his arm up, reached with straining fingers for his pocket, and pushed down. It was like using flesh to prop a heavy object. But seconds later, his hand—bruised and strangely numb—was inside his pocket.

With all his strength, he forced his hand to open, to grasp the remote-control device that was in that pocket. But he did not immediately activate its first stage. "Wait," he thought, "till the Karn gets some distance away."

He sat there; rather, he remained in his squeezed position, breathing with difficulty, conscious of a developing exhaustion. That brought alarm. Was it possible that his body could wear itself out at four g's, *sitting?*

Yet if he killed Dzing at once, that would leave him alone

with Browne and his minions, facing a sentence of death which Browne had not rescinded.

And if he merely stopped the acceleration, that would bring the Karn robot racing back to find out what had happened.

. . . Nonpermissible, yet how avoid it . . . ?

As Lesbee reasoned it, the longer he could hold off final action the better his chance of learning vital information. For example, the question of how Dzing had speeded up the ship's drive had to be correctly understood. With so much new force in motion, an unconsidered move could kill people instantly, might even damage the ship itself.

With that thought, he began a careful examination of the big board in front of him. The minutes dragged; and still he continued his study. The extreme tiredness that rapidly grew on him began to be his main problem. He kept dozing, and he would awaken with the shocked realization that time had gone by.

But presently he understood.

The acceleration was twelve gravities; the artificial-gravity force was eight gravities. The gap between the two—four gravities—was the pressure that was affecting them so severely.

Lesbee had a sense of awe. This was a new, unheard-of technique. It meant that drastic changes had been made by remote-control mental action in the drive and the artificial-gravity coils.

Hitherto the use of artificial gravity at the same time as acceleration had not been possible. There simply wasn't enough power available. But Dzing had rectified that by creating a vast new power source; the rapid ejection and expansion of particles multiplied the usable energy by some huge amount; theoretically, it was tens of thousands of times greater. In practice, of course, at low speeds, it was only a few hundred times greater.

But there was enough power for all conceivable contingencies.

Sitting there, breathing in that labored fashion, Lesbee felt the fantastic reality of the universe. During all this slow century of flight through space, the *Hope of Man* had had the potential for this vastly greater velocity.

"And Dr. Tellier missed it," he thought.

Missed it! And so a shipload of human beings had wandered for generations through the black deeps of interstellar space.

Lesbee thought, "The moment I activate the first of the three stages of my little control device, Dzing will lose *his* control of the drive and of the artificial gravity."

Unfortunately, it would probably also send him racing back to the alternate control board to find out what had happened.

Lesbee realized he could not take any chances with that at all. He would have to activate the Karn's self-destruct system with Stage Three of his little control device. And what bothered him about that was, paradoxically, that the robot was a protection for him.

The moment the creature was destroyed, the total power that Browne had aboard the ship would be reasserted. Lesbee thought, "If I can gain just a few minutes time here, while I maneuver around with Browne—"

He thought about that for a moment longer. And then, because he dared not delay, he pressed the first button and then the third one.

Instantly, his body sagged in its belt, weightless.

Lesbee held himself alert, listening. But if there was an explosion anywhere on the ship, its repercussion failed to reach him.

He thought, appalled, "Good God, can it be the destruct system didn't work?"

The panicky feeling that came subsided before a new, urgent problem. Across the room Browne was climbing groggily to his feet.

He muttered: ". . . better get back to . . . control chair. . . ."

He had taken only a few uncertain steps when a realization seemed to strike him. He looked up, and stared wildly at Lesbee. "Oh!" he said. It was a gasp of horrified understanding.

There was no time any more to think about Dzing. As he slapped a complex of tractor beams on Browne, Lesbee said, "That's right. You're looking at your enemy. Let's have that completely understood, because we haven't got much time. Now, I want to ask you some questions."

Browne was pale. He said huskily, "I did what any lawful government does in an emergency. I dealt with treason summarily, taking time only to find out what it consisted of."

The explanation was a meaningless bit of nonsense, in view of the history of the ship. But Lesbee did not pause to argue. He had a tense consciousness of working against time. It was outrageous that he had to fight both Browne's forces and Dzing, but that was the fact; and so, hastily, he swung Browne over in front of him, and took his blaster.

Lesbee felt better when he had the weapon. But there was still another danger. Without turning, he spoke at the screen that connected directly with the bridge: "*Mr.* Miller, are you there?"

There was no answer.

Lesbee said to Browne, "Tell Miller not to attempt pre-emption. Any attempt by him to take over control means I'll use this blaster on you. *Got that Miller?*" His voice was uncompromising.

Again, there was no reply.

Browne said uneasily, "He may have been knocked unconscious."

Lesbee ardently hoped so, but there was no time for verification. For a few, vital, uninterrupted minutes now, he needed Browne's knowledge.

17

It was a moment for a combination of deviousness and frankness. Lesbee would have given a lot to be able to send out a single question over the speaker system. He wanted desperately to ask if there had been an explosion anywhere on the ship.

But if there had been—if Dzing were destroyed—that knowledge would apprise the Browne forces that they had only a lone human being to deal with; and they would act promptly.

And so, he dared not try to verify that vital information.

But there were several things that Browne *could* help him on, and *might*, during these tense minutes when he himself felt threatened.

Lesbee said urgently: "What bothers me is how that creature could walk out of here and not be affected by the acceleration? It's impossible, yet he did it."

He finished with a lie: "I find myself reluctant to act against the creature until we have an understanding of what it was he did."

He had lowered the big man to the floor, and now he took some of the tension from the tractor beam, but did not release the power. Browne stood in apparent deep thought. Finally, he nodded. "All right, I know what happened."

"Tell me!"

Browne changed the subject, said in a deliberate tone, "What are you going to do with me?"

Lesbee stared at him disbelievingly. "You're going to withhold this information?"

Browne said, "What else can I do? Till I know my fate, I have nothing to lose."

To Lesbee the words brought brief cynicism. "What's this?" he said satirically. "Could this be a scheme to utilize alien creatures to destroy human beings? Are you putting your own safety above that of the ship and its mission? Don't you think this justifies summary execution?"

The tone must have alarmed Browne, for he said quickly, "Look, there's no need for you to conspire any more. What you really want is to go home, isn't it? Don't you see, with this new method of acceleration, we can make it to Earth in a few months."

He stopped. He seemed uncertain.

Lesbee said angrily, "Who are you trying to fool? We're a dozen light-years in actual distance from Earth. You mean years, not months."

Browne hesitated. "All right, a few years. But at least not a lifetime. So if you'll promise not to scheme against me further, I'll promise—"

"*You'll* promise!" Lesbee spoke savagely. He had been taken aback by Browne's instant attempt to blackmail. But the momentary sense of defeat was gone. He knew with stubborn rage that he would stand for no nonsense.

He said in an uncompromising tone, "Mr. Browne, twenty seconds after I stop speaking, you start talking. I mean it."

Browne said, "Are you going to kill me? That's the only thing I want reassurance on. Look"—his voice appealed—"we don't have to fight any more. We can go home. Don't you see? The long madness is just about over. Nobody has to die. But quick, man, destroy that creature with your remote-control method!"

Lesbee hesitated. What the other was saying was at least partly true. His words so far included an attempt to make twelve years sound like twelve weeks or, at most, twelve months. But the fact was, it *was* a short period compared to the century-long journey which, at one time, had been the only possibility.

He thought, "Am I going to kill him?"

It was hard to believe that he would, under the circumstances. But if not death, what then? He sat there, uncertain. The vital seconds went by, and he could see no solution. He thought finally, in desperation: "I'll have to give in for the moment."

"I'll promise you this," he said. "If you can figure out how I can feel safe in a ship commanded by you, I'll give your plan consideration. And now, mister, start talking."

Browne nodded. "I accept that promise."

Browne went on, "There are two possible explanations, and naturally I prefer the more commonplace one. That is, I postulate that this robot used some kind of energy flows, like a balance of tractor and pressor beams. He used this in the same instantaneous, or rapid, feedback system that you and I use in our muscles to balance ourselves when we walk under normal gravity."

"What is the second explanation?" Lesbee asked.

"That takes us beyond normal response and normal energy situations. When we last saw the robot, the appearance he presented was of an object for which the entire phenomenon of inertia had been suspended. If this were true, then we are observing a big event, indeed. To understand it, we'd have to consider light-speed theories and, particularly, the Lorentz-Fitzgerald Contraction Theory. At the speed of light, mass becomes infinite but size is zero. Thus, matter ceases instantly to be subject to inertia as we know it. There is no other condition in the universe where that can happen naturally. Dzing has somehow created the condition artificially—if this second explanation is the true one."

Lesbee said doubtfully, "I'm inclined to accept the tractor-pressor explanation. Is there any way we could determine which method he used?"

Browne could think of no method for determining it after the event. "If it was a combination of energy flows, then it probably registered on the board at the time. And it will show again when he comes into the room."

That, Lesbee realized, would be a little late to be useful. He asked helplessly, "Is there anything we need to learn from this creature?"

"We've already learned it," said Browne. "This thing has a casual control of energy and an understanding of space time that is far ahead of us scientifically. Therefore, we have no business in this sun system. So let's get out of here as fast as we can."

Lesbee was remembering how all the Karn on the lifeboat had pretended to be affected by inertia, when they evidently had not been.

Aloud, he said, "Maybe your second explanation does cover it better."

Browne shook his head. "No, he'd have been here within instants, if that was what he could do. There's a state of compressed time at light-speed."

"How do you mean?"

Browne was uneasy. "Let's not waste time on an intellectual discussion," he said.

"I want to know what you mean."

"It's condensed time. He would have a time ratio, in relation to us, of hundreds to one. Ten minutes for us could be only a second for him."

"Then he should have been here by now, if that's what he could do?"

"That's what I've been trying to tell you."

Lesbee had to fight to hold back his excitement. The thought in his mind was that by pressing Button Three immediately after Button One, he had prevented that kind of instantaneous return by the Karn.

He thought, "And I did it without even knowing how deadly dangerous the situation was, because I was logical, because I didn't want to take any chances."

He felt a great joy in himself.

"For God's sake, Lesbee—"

Lesbee's elation faded as rapidly as it had come, for Browne was as great a danger as ever.

Lesbee gazed at the man gloomily.

"For God's sake, Lesbee," said Browne, "that thing must be practically back here. Tell me what you want me to agree to, and I'll do it."

Lesbee said, "I think we ought to have an election."

"I agree," said Browne instantly. "You set it up." He broke off. "And now release me from these tractors, and let's act."

Lesbee gazed at the man's face, saw there the same openness of countenance, the same frank, honest look that had preceded the execution order, and he thought, "What can he do?"

He considered many possibilities, and thought finally, desperately, "He's got the advantage of superior knowledge—the most undefeatable weapon in the world. The only thing I can really hope to use against it in the final issue is *my* knowledge of a multitude of technician-level details."

But—what could Browne do against him?

Lesbee said unhappily, "Before I free you, I want to lift you over to Mindel. When I do, you get his blaster for me."

"Sure," said Browne casually.

A few minutes later he handed Mindel's gun over to Lesbee. So that wasn't it.

Lesbee thought: "There's Miller on the bridge—can it be that Miller flashed him a ready signal when my back was turned to the board?"

Perhaps, like Browne, Miller had been temporarily incapacitated during the period of acceleration. It was vital that he find out Miller's present capability.

Lesbee tripped the intercom between the two boards. The rugged, lined face of the first officer showed large on the screen. Lesbee could see the outlines of the bridge behind the man and, beyond, the starry blackness of space. Lesbee said courteously, "Mr. Miller, how did you make out during the acceleration?"

"It caught me by surprise, Captain. I really got a battering. I think I was out for a while. But I'm all right now."

"Good," said Lesbee. "As you probably heard, Captain Browne and I have come to an agreement, and we are now going to destroy the creature that is loose on the ship. Stand by!"

Cynically, he broke the connection.

Miller was there all right, waiting. But the question was still, what could Miller do? The answer was, of course, that Miller could pre-empt. And—Lesbee asked himself—what could *that* do?

Suddenly, he had the answer.

He now understood Browne's plan. They were waiting for

Lesbee to let his guard down for a moment. Then Miller would take over, cut off the tractor beam from Browne, and seize Lesbee with it.

For the two officers it was vital that Lesbee not have the time to fire the blaster at Browne. Lesbee thought: "It's the only thing they can be worried about, so far as I'm concerned." And as soon as Lesbee was dead, or under control, Browne would grab the mechanism out of his pocket, and activate Stage Three—which would destroy Dzing.

Their plan, as Lesbee saw it, had only one flaw. Now that he had deduced what it was, he could turn it against them.

He realized that he had preparations to make quickly, before Browne got suspicious of his delay.

He turned to the board and switched on the intercom. "People," he said, "strap yourselves in again. Help those who were injured to do the same. We may have another emergency. You all have about a minute, I think, but don't waste any of it."

He cut off that intercom, and activated the closed-circuit intercom of the technical stations. He said: "Special instructions to technical personnel. Listen carefully. Did any of you hear an explosion about ten minutes ago?"

He had an answer to that within moments after he had finished speaking. A man's twangy voice came: "This is Dan. There was an explosion in the corridor near me—seems longer ago than ten minutes."

Lesbee restrained his excitement. "Where?" he asked.

"D—four—nineteen."

Lesbee pressed the viewer buttons, and a moment later found himself gazing along a corridor that looked stove in. Wall, ceiling, floor—everything—was a mass of twisted metal.

No question, Dzing had been blown apart. There was no other possible explanation for such destruction.

Relieved, but aware again that his greatest personal danger remained, Lesbee set up Stage Two of the little device in his pocket in relation to the alternate control board. Then he turned and faced Browne.

The older man seemed uncertain as to what had happened. "What was all that?" he asked.

Lesbee explained that Dzing was destroyed.

"Oh!" Browne seemed to consider that. "That was clever of you not to reveal it," he said finally.

"I wasn't sure," Lesbee said. "This ship is really sound-proofed. The explosion didn't reach us here."

Browne seemed to accept that.

Lesbee said, "If you'll wait a moment while I put away this gun, I'll carry out my part of the bargain."

But when he had put the blaster away, he paused out of pity.

He had been thinking about what Browne had said, earlier: that the trip to Earth might require only a few months. The officer had backed away from that statement, but it had been bothering Lesbee ever since.

If it were true, then, indeed, nobody needed to die.

He said quickly, "What was your reason for saying that the journey home would only take—well—less than a year?"

"It's the tremendous time compression near light-speed," Browne explained eagerly. "The distance, as you pointed out, is over twelve light-years. But with this new principle of acceleration, we can work up a time ratio of 300, 400, or 500 to one, and we'll actually make the trip in less than a month. When I first started to say that, I could see that the figures were incomprehensible to you in your tense mood. In fact, I could scarcely believe them myself."

Lesbee said, staggered, "We can get back to the solar system in a few weeks—my God!" He broke off, said urgently, "Look, I accept you as commander. We don't need an election. The status quo is good enough for any short period of time. Do you agree?"

"Of course," said Browne. "That's the point I've been trying to make."

As he spoke, his face was utterly guileless.

Lesbee gazed at that mask of innocence and he thought hopelessly, "What's wrong? Why isn't he really agreeing? Is it because he doesn't want to lose his comand so quickly?"

Sitting there, unhappily fighting for the other's life, he tried to place himself mentally in the position of the commander of a vessel, tried to look at the prospect of a return to Earth from the other's point of view. It was hard to picture. But presently it seemed to him that he understood.

He said gently, feeling his way, "It would be kind of a shame to return without having made a successful landing anywhere. With this new speed, we could visit a dozen sun systems, and still get home in a year."

The look that came into Browne's face for a fleeting moment told Lesbee that he had penetrated to the thought in the man's mind.

The next instant Browne was shaking his head vigorously. "This is no time for side excursions," he said. "We'll leave explorations of new star systems to future expeditions. The people of this ship have served their term. We go straight home."

Browne's face was now completely relaxed. His blue eyes shone with truth and sincerity.

There was nothing further that Lesbee could say. The gulf between Browne and himself could not be bridged.

The commander had to kill his rival so that he might finally return to Earth and report that the mission of the *Hope of Man* had been accomplished.

18

Lesbee used the tractor beam to push Browne about six feet from him. There he set him down, and released him from the beam. With the same deliberateness, he drew his hand away from the tractor controls, and swung his chair around so that his back was to the board. Thus he rendered himself completely defenseless.

It was the moment of vulnerability.

Browne leaped at him, yelling: "Miller—pre-empt!"

First Officer Miller obeyed the command of his captain.

As the bridge control board took over, a sequence of control exchanges was set in motion.

The alternate control board was removed from the circuit.

The rerouted electric current opened and closed relays, in accordance with the physics of current flow.

The two control boards were so perfectly synchronized that the one which took over always continued what the other had had set up on it. Normally, therefore, nothing could go wrong during pre-emption.

But in this instance, the alternate control board had one of its controls subordinated to the tiny device in Lesbee's pocket. At the moment, that powerful little gadget was holding in check twelve g's of drive and eight g's of artificial gravity . . . *in reverse,* exactly as Lesbee had reprogrammed them when he pressed the Stage Two Button.

When the bridge took over, the drive and the artificial gravity resumed their function instantly.

The *Hope of Man*—instantly—decelerated at a four-g gap speed.

Lesbee took the blow of that abrupt slowdown, partly against his back and partly against his right side, with the sturdy rear of the chair as his principal support.

It was a wholly adequate support.

But Browne was caught off balance. He had been coming at Lesbee from an angle. The enormous impact of the deceleration flung him at this angle straight at the control board. He struck it with an audible thud and stuck to it as if he were glued there.

A cut-off relay, which Lesbee had also preprogrammed through the alternate control board, now shut off the engines as suddenly as they had started. During the weightlessness that followed, Browne's body worked itself free and slid down to the dais.

There was discoloration at a dozen spots on the uniform. As Lesbee stared, fascinated, blood seeped through.

19

"Are you going to hold an election?" Tellier asked.

The big ship, under Lesbee's command, had turned back and had picked up his friends. The lifeboat itself, with the remaining Karn still aboard, was put into orbit around Alta III and abandoned.

The two young men were sitting now in the captain's cabin.

After the question had been asked, Lesbee leaned back in

his chair and closed his eyes. He didn't need to examine his total resistance to the suggestion. He had already savored the feeling that command brought.

Almost from the moment of Browne's death, he had observed himself having the same thoughts that Browne had voiced—among many others, the reasons why elections were not advisable aboard a spaceship. He waited now while Ilsa, one of his three wives—she being the younger of the two widows of Browne—poured wine for them and went softly out. Then he laughed grimly.

"My good friend," he said, "we're all lucky that time is so compressed at the speed of light. At a time ratio of five hundred to one, any further exploration we do will require only a few months or years at most. And so, I don't think we can afford to take the chance of defeating at an election the only person who understands the details of the new acceleration method. Till I decide exactly how much exploration we shall do, I shall keep our speed capabilities a secret. But I did, and do, think one other person should know where I have this information documented. Naturally, I am selecting First Officer Armand Tellier."

He raised his glass. "As soon as I have the full account written, you shall have a copy."

"Thank you, Captain," the young man said. But he was thoughtful as he sipped his wine. He went on finally, "Captain, I think you'd feel a lot better if you held an election. I'm sure you could win it."

Lesbee laughed tolerantly, shook his head. "I'm afraid you don't understand the dynamics of government," he said. "There's no record in history of a person, who actually had control, handing it over."

He finished with the casual confidence of absolute power: "I'm not going to be presumptuous enough to fight a precedent like that."

He was sitting there, smiling cynically, when the buzzer of the front door of the captain's cabin sounded in the adjoining room. Lesbee was aware of one of his wives going to the door and opening it. Surprisingly, then, there was not another sound. No greeting, no acknowledgment; total silence.

Lesbee thought, "Whoever it is, has handed her a note."

The instant analysis ended a feeling of uneasiness. He was about to settle back in his chair, when a man's rough voice came quietly from behind him.

"All right, Mr. Lesbee, your take-over is ended and ours is beginning."

Lesbee froze. Then, turning, stared with an awful sinking sensation at the armed men who were crowding in behind the man who had spoken. He didn't know any of the men but he saw that they were laborers, garden men, and kitchen help. People of whose existence he had never been more than vaguely aware.

The leader of the group spoke again.

"Gourdy is my name, Mr. Lesbee, and we're taking over—these men and I—because we want to go home, back to Earth. . . . Be careful, and you and your friends won't be hurt—"

Lesbee sighed with relief as those final words were spoken. All was not lost.

20

Gourdy was thirty-four when he led the revolt that overthrew Lesbee V. He was a thick-built, small man with very black eyes, and he had been brought up with the daily memory that his father had led an abortive rebellion. Long ago, he had determined that he would carry out his father's ideals to the death, if necessary. He had a courage that derived from hatred and a shrewdness that had gradually developed from his skeptical attitude toward any and every bit of information that had ever come down to the lower decks from above. He had instantly spotted as false the apparent friendship of Browne and Lesbee, and recognized it as a struggle and not a collaboration. Far more important, he had seen that this was the opportunity for which he himself had been waiting.

He moved into the captain's cabin, and because it was all new to him he took nothing for granted. What was visible to his keen, wondering gaze merely served as an inducement to explore what was not visible. Thus, in raising the metal floor to make sure there was nothing under it that could be used against him, he discovered the detectaphone system by which it was possible to listen in to every room of the big ship. And when he had some of the walls broken open, he found the labyrinth of passageways by which technicians like Lesbee had kept track of tens of thousands of miles of wiring.

For the first time, he was able to reconstruct how his father had been killed—from such a passageway—while apparently safe behind the barred doors of a storeroom. The finding of these and other hidden chambers took some of the magic out of the scientific realities of the ship. Gourdy reasoned that a leader need not himself be a scientist to run the ship, but he had a strong feeling that he would probably have to kill a few people, before the scientific community would accept him and his untrained helpers.

From the beginning, his extreme suspicion and rage motivated him to act with the exact rationality required for a people's revolution to be successful. He had every doubtful person put down in the laboring quarters and barred from the upper floors till further notice. He reasoned that all decisions relating to key men would have far-reaching consequences. Although a large number of persons was involved, he personally interviewed each man.

Most of the scientists seemed resigned to working with him. Many of them expressed relief that someone was finally in command of the ship who really would set course for Earth. All of these Gourdy listed to return to their regular duties under the system he had worked out, whereby never more than one third of any staff would be admitted to the laboratories at one time.

About a score of men made him uneasy in some way: their manner, something they said, the kind of work they did. These he classified in a special category. It would be some time before they were allowed to the upper levels, for any reason.

All of Browne's and Lesbee's officers he told bluntly that he planned to make use of their knowledge but that, until further notice, they would not be admitted "upstairs," except one at a time and then under guard.

Of the entire group of nearly two hundred persons, only one technician and two minor scientists proved resistant. They were openly contemptuous of the new government of the *Hope of Man*. All three offered Gourdy direct insults as he questioned them. They sneered at his clothes, at his way of speaking, and swore at him.

Gourdy parried the invective thoughtfully. He was not suspicious or afraid that the three were part of a conspiracy; they were too obvious. He surmised extreme unawareness, but he had a hardness of purpose that rejected sympathy or understanding. He saw with grim satisfaction that here were his examples.

He killed all three men and announced the killings over the public-address system, about an hour before the next sleep period.

That done—*all* the preliminaries done—he ordered Lesbee to be brought up to him. And so, a few minutes later, for the first time since the take-over, the two men faced each other. In a cool, incisive voice, Gourdy told his prisoner, "I thought I'd keep you to the last—"

He didn't explain why, and for Lesbee, now that the executions had taken place, it didn't matter. It was too late. Sitting there, with the other's intense black eyes staring at him, Lesbee silently cursed himself. He had actually had the fleeting thought earlier that this man might do something drastic, had actually thought of sending a message to Gourdy asking him not to do anything irrevocable without a discussion. But the new captain might have insisted on knowing why, and so he had held back.

The sad truth was, he had welcomed the delay over his own interrogation, wanted the time to make up his own mind. In the end he had decided that no one, least of all himself, had anything to gain from a prolonged voyage with Gourdy in command. And so he had planned to tell about the light-speed effect.

The murder of the three men changed that purpose. Now, he dared not tell, for, obviously, Gourdy would be unwilling to return to Earth, where a court might take a dim view of the killings.

As a cover-up for his genuine state of shock, Lesbee adopted the scientific pose. Complete control by nonscientists was a terrible mistake; that was his argument. He thereupon proposed that his forces and Gourdy's work together to achieve the journey to Earth. He suggested a captain's board consisting of Gourdy, two of Gourdy's henchmen, Tellier, and himself.

"That," he said, "will give you a three-to-two voting majority, but will provide a stable communication line with two persons who know how the ship works and who were also victims of the previous hierarchy."

Lesbee had no real expectation that Gourdy would accept such a compromise. He did hope it would create a softening attitude in the man.

If so, there was no immediate sign of it. Gourdy did not believe in boards, or councils, or split commands, and he proceeded to make this clear. The ship had one commander, himself. All persons aboard would either co-operate with him to the best of their ability or they would be punished according to their dereliction. Death would be the penalty for any kind of severe disloyalty or sabotage.

The statement of policy was so harshly uttered that Lesbee felt abrupt fear for his own safety. Recovering, he quietly promised to obey Gourdy's orders.

The small man stared at him for many seconds after he had spoken. Then his manner changed to a kind of surly cordiality. "Let's drink on that, hey!" he said.

He poured wine into two glasses, handed one to Lesbee, and raised the other in a toast. What he said was, "Mr. Lesbee, I kept your interview to the last because the fact is you're probably the only expert aboard I can trust—in spite of you being the one I took over from."

They sipped the wine, Lesbee uneasy but as convinced as ever that he couldn't tell the other man about the nearness of Earth, Gourdy a little puzzled by something in Lesbee's manner but satisfied that his selection of Lesbee was logical.

He grew expansive, said slyly, "In a couple of weeks, if you behave, I'll bring you up to a cabin and send your real wife to live with you." He added, "Although I haven't done anything about it yet, I'm probably gonna have to keep those other two women. My own wife—believe it or not—insists on it. Startled me, because she used to be so damned jealous down below. Not here. I guess"—he frowned—"being on a ship like this is not good for a woman. Makes her feel empty inside. She's already blasted me with a kind of crazy hysteria about it. I think she has some kind of feeling that I won't really be captain till I take over the captain's wives. But don't worry, it won't include yours."

Lesbee remained silent. He sat considering the possibilities that the emotional instability of the women aboard might be due to voyage conditions. Then he realized it was of little consequence.

Gourdy was continuing unhappily: "Makes it kind of awkward. Down below, we were against all this multiple-wife stuff. We'll sure look like phonies if we just grab for women the moment we're in control." Once more, he frowned. Then he straightened, raised his glass. "I'll think about the other ladies later. Here's to your wife."

After they had drunk the wine, his manner changed again. He put his glass down. He said curtly, "Let's get this ship headed for home."

He led the way to the auxiliary control room. "No bridge yet for you," he said, then warned, "don't try any tricks now."

Lesbee walked over to the control board in a deliberate fashion. The question in his mind was: If he simply set the two dials and threw two switches, would Gourdy get the idea that he could handle this himself? On the other hand, if he made it seem too complex, the man might have someone else—Miller or Mindel—check on everything he did.

In the end he did only two unnecessary things. Since Gourdy wanted to know the meaning of his moves, he explained in double-talk what he had done and why. A few minutes later he had the acceleration at twelve g's, and the artificial gravity at eleven, thus leaving a gap of one gravity, exactly the same as on Earth.

The programming completed, Lesbee stood by while Gourdy announced the action over the public-address system, ending with, "We're going home. Yes, my friends, our destination is Earth itself."

He instructed: ". . . sleep in your acceleration belts, since we plan to increase acceleration during the night."

Lesbee listened, ashamed and embarrassed. Such an "increase" in acceleration merely meant that he would widen the gap between the drive thrust and the artificial gravity, which was unnecessary. Since Dzing had "adjusted" the coils in the engines and the synchronizers in the artificial gravity system, they could be stepped up simultaneously to maintain a steady one gravity, no matter what the rate of increase.

However, this had not hitherto been true; so he would not let it be true now. It was to his advantage to immobilize people.

Listening to the man, Lesbee thought with gloomy cynicism: "The ridiculous truth is, the moment he discovers how near to Earth we actually are, with this new engine control, he'll kill me out of hand."

21

As the days and weeks passed, he realized he was the only technical person who was being permitted to go into the two control rooms and in the engine room. It became apparent that whatever was finally done would be up to him.

His brain seethed with schemes. And yet the only possible thing he could actually do occurred to him the first day. He kept rejecting it, saw too many flaws in it, felt its danger. But on the twenty-sixth day he told the idea to Tellier. It was one of those rare moments when he was certain he was not being spied on: Gourdy had left the lower floors only moments before and was obviously en route somewhere and not listening in, and so Lesbee could speak freely.

He grew aware of his friend's dismay. "Exceed the speed of light!" Tellier echoed. "Are you serious?"

Lesbee said defensively, "We won't actually do it. But I've got to get it programmed for and in reserve. He's a killer—don't ever forget that."

Tellier groaned. "If this is the best you can think of, we're in trouble."

Lesbee explained earnestly: "At our present rate of acceleration, we'll come to 99.999998 per cent of light-speed in about three days. When that happens, it will require only two ship hours to jump many light-years, all the way to the solar system. So we've got to stop accelerating or we'll zoom right out of the galaxy. Now, how do I do all this without letting on to Gourdy who expects the journey to Earth to take thirty years?"

A strange look came into Tellier's thin, intellectual face. He grabbed Lesbee's arm, said hoarsely, "John—during these three days, why don't you just fix up one of the lifeboats, shut off our engines, scramble the light system, and in the confusion you and me get off?"

Lesbee was taken aback. Leave the ship! Although he considered that the idea was not practicable, he was astonished that such a thought had never occurred to him. But he realized why it hadn't. The ship was a part of his life and not a separate thing at all.

He said finally, thinking out loud, "That would have to be some fix-up on that lifeboat. It takes a long time to slow down. What I figure is, when we get close to light-speed, I'll juggle the gravity and the acceleration, and then get permission to cut off."

He stood, scowling, considering. Tellier wanted to know what was bothering him.

Lesbee realized he couldn't explain to any other person the difficulty of dealing with Gourdy. Haltingly, he tried to describe the paranoic suspicionness of the man. He said, "He knows enough about the controls to know when they're in operation. Teaching him was my only method of preventing him from having someone check on the engines. If I go to him—" He stopped again, picturing the possibilities, then said, "It's so vital I can't take the chance that he won't do it now."

"So?" Tellier wanted to know.

It seemed to Lesbee that he must inform Captain Gourdy that the engines were not functioning properly and get permission to cut off the drives before the ship attained light-speed. He argued the point earnestly. "But I'll program it so that if he gets suspicious and bars me from upstairs, then, in due course, the engines will start again and take us across the light-speed barrier, and since it will look as if I had predicted trouble, Gourdy will trust me again."

He grew aware that Tellier was gazing at him admiringly. "You really do have a mind for intrigue, don't you?" He added anxiously, "But if he's not suspicious, you'll keep us on this side of light?"

"Of course. Do you think I'm crazy! As an emergency precaution, believe it or not, I've already activated the old sensor equipment for zeroing in, first on the solar system, then on Earth."

The conversation ended with an agreement as to which airlock they would use for their escape and under what circumstances they would rendezvous there.

Later that afternoon, Lesbee programmed for the additional patterned acceleration, using electromagnetic controls exclusively. It had occurred to him that it would be unwise to trust any mere mechanical device at near light-speed.

The action taken, he went to Gourdy and brazenly made his statement about the drives, that he would have to shut them off to see what was wrong.

Gourdy was instantly anxious. "But we'll keep coasting along while you're checking them?" he asked.

"Of course," said Lesbee. "We'd come to this condition presently anyway, where we have to shut off the engines to conserve fuel, and coast. But that's still months away."

Lesbee had once toyed with the idea of using that natural sequence. But it had seemed to him that the longer he remained at the mercy of Gourdy, the more impossible his plan would be. Even now, at the stepped-up rate that he had used, simply coasting would require a disconcertingly high number of years to make the journey. It was unfortunate but only within light yards and light feet per second of light-speed were the enormous relative speeds attainable.

They were standing on the bridge. Against the backdrop of unending, star-dotted night. Gourdy's eyes were narrowed. He was evidently having those second thoughts of his. Lesbee felt the tension mounting in his stomach.

Gourdy said, "Does this trouble have an emergency look?"

"Captain, the sooner I check on what's wrong, the better. But it could wait till the sleep period."

"Well—" Gourdy seemed to be coming to a decision. "I guess it's all right. What about the gravity?"

"It'll have to go off," Lesbee lied.

"Then wait till after dinner. If you haven't heard from me in an hour before the sleep period, program for engine shut-off during the night. I'll announce it and tell people to sleep in their safety belts. How long do you figure it will take?"

"A couple of days."

Gourdy was silent, frowning. He said at last: "It'll be a nuisance, though I guess we'll do it. But wait, like I said. O.K.?"

"O.K."

Lesbee dared not say one extra word. He went down the steps, heart in mouth, and he was greatly relieved, while he was in the commissary, to hear Gourdy announce the forthcoming slowdown over the public-address system.

Unfortunately for Lesbee's peace of mind, as Gourdy turned away from the microphone, he found himself remembering that Lesbee had been trained as a technician and not as an engineer. He doubted if Lesbee were really qualified to repair or evaluate the need for repair of the atomic drive.

The question did not include any suspicion of Lesbee's motives. He simply asked himself: Was it wise to trust a technician with something so vital to the future of the ship?

After these thoughts had matured for a few minutes, Gourdy ordered the late Captain Browne's former first officer, Miller, to be brought to the auxiliary control room.

He said to Miller quite simply, "I have reason to believe the engines are not operating properly. Would you check and give me your opinion?"

For Miller it was a moment of dilemma. He had been an officer his entire adult lifetime. He despised Gourdy and he disliked Lesbee but, most of all, he hated living on the lower decks. During the incident with the robot at Alta, he had been unconscious while Lesbee and Browne had had their discussion about the speed of light. Accordingly, he had not understood those later snatches of conversation in which those two angry men had referred to the Lorentz-Fitzgerald theory. At no time, then or since, had he been aware that the ship was traveling faster than its best previous speed.

And this was his first time near the controls since Lesbee's take-over. He studied the dials on the big board with genuine interest. It did not take him long to decide that the engines were operating perfectly. In fact, remembering some old manuals that showed theoretical optimums, he had the feeling that on the whole, for a reason that was not clear, the drive was working more smoothly than at any previous time that he had seen it.

Realizing this, he deduced with the contempt of the engineer for the technician that Lesbee had somehow misread the data. His dilemma was: how could he utilize his superior knowledge to get back into a position of greater importance? Should he back Lesbee and get in on the unnecessary repair job? Or should he here and now begin a struggle for position with that individual?

He decided on the struggle. "After all," he thought, "this is every man for himself."

At the precise moment that he made his decision, his roving glance lighted on the velocity indicators, which were on a separate instrument board to one side. The needles showed an extreme configuration that he had never seen before. Frowning, Miller walked over, mentally calculating a rough approximation of what the figures meant. His puffy face quivered. He turned.

"Captain Gourdy," he said, "a lot of things are suddenly beginning to make sense to me."

Afterwards, when he had explained to Gourdy what he meant, and after he had finally been returned below, Miller sought out the unsuspecting Lesbee, and said cockily, "Captain Gourdy just had me look at the engines."

Lesbee silently absorbed the terrible shock of that and, being acutely conscious of being spied on, said in a steady voice, "I was thinking of asking the captain to have you verify my findings."

Miller's response was rough-toned. "O.K., if you want to pretend. Let me tell you, all kinds of things fell into place when I saw those velocity indicators. I never did understand, when Browne was killed." He smiled knowingly. "Pretty smart, getting almost up to the speed of light, never letting on."

It seemed to Lesbee that his face must be the color of lead. He could have hit the other man, standing there with his round brown eyes full of foolish triumph. He stepped close to Miller, said in a low, vicious voice, "You stupid fool! Don't you realize that Gourdy can't go to Earth? We're all dead men!"

There was brief satisfaction, then, in seeing the expression of horrible awareness take form on Miller's face. Lesbee turned away, sick at heart. And he was not surprised a few minutes later when he received a call to report to the captain's cabin.

As it developed, he didn't get all the way there. En route he was arrested and placed in one of the ship's prison cages. It was there that Gourdy came to him. His coal-black eyes stared at Lesbee through the bars. He said grimly, "All right, Mr. Lesbee, tell me all about the speed of this ship."

Lesbee took the chance that his conversation with Miller had not been monitored—and pretended to be totally unaware of what Gourdy was talking about. It seemed to him that his only hope was to convince this terrible little man that he was absolutely innocent.

Gourdy was taken aback. And because the entire situation was so fantastic, he was half-inclined to believe Lesbee. He could imagine that a technician had simply not grasped what had happened.

But he also found himself inexorably analyzing the other possibility: that Lesbee had known the facts and had planned to stop the ship, get off, and leave those who remained aboard to solve the mystery for themselves. The mere contemplation of it enraged him.

"O.K. for you!" he said balefully. "If you won't talk, I have no alternative but to treat you like a liar and a saboteur."

But he returned to his cabin, shocked and unhappy, no longer a well and confident man, conscious that the new development threatened him only and that he must act quickly.

With his strong sense of personal danger, Gourdy let his feelings guide him. The need to take all necessary precautions—that was first. And so, as the sleep period began, he led an expedition down to the lower decks and arrested eighteen persons, including Miller and Tellier. All eighteen were placed under separate lock and key.

Gourdy spent the second hour of the sleep period in a sleepless soul-searching, and there was presently no doubt in his mind that his actions—particular the executions—had been geared to a thirty-year journey.

"I might as well face the truth," he thought. "I can't take the chance of returning to Earth."

As he planned it then, he would have Lesbee slow the ship to a point where it *would* require thirty years to get to the solar system. Then, when he had worked out a good propaganda reason for doing so, he would execute Lesbee, Miller, Mindel, and the other real suspects. The reason, of course, would be basically that they were plotting to take over the ship, but the details needed to be carefully thought about so that people would either believe the story or at least be half-inclined to believe it.

He was still lying there an hour later, considering exactly what he would do and say when, under him, the ship jumped as if it had been struck. There followed the unmistakable sensation of acceleration.

Lesbee had been tensely awake as the fateful hour approached. On the dot the forward surge caught him and pressed him back against the belt that partly encased his body. According to his programming, the preliminary gap between acceleration and artificial gravity would be three g's, enough to hold everyone down until they crossed light-speed.

He felt a sickening fear as he realized that at this very instant time and space must already be telescoping at an astro-
nomical rate.

"Hurry, hurry!" he thought weakly.

Although there was no way of sensing it that he knew of,
since both acceleration and artificial gravity were increasing
together, he braced himself for the fantastically compressed
period light-inches before and beyond light-speed. His hope
was that it would pass by in a tiny fraction of an instant.

The bracing action was like a signal. As he lay there, expecting agony, he had a fantasy that was gone so quickly that
he forgot what it was. Then another fantasy, a face—never
seen before—instantly gone. Then he began to see images.
They were all going backward: himself and other people
aboard, actually walking backward as on a film in reverse.
The scenes were fleeting; thousands streamed by and,
presently, there were images from his childhood.

The pictures faded into confusion. He was aware of a
floating sensation, not pleasant, but not the agony he had expected. And then—

He must have blacked out.

22

Averill Hewitt hung up the phone, and repeated aloud the
message he had just been given: "Your spaceship, *Hope of
Man,* is entering the atmosphere of Earth."

The words echoed and re-echoed in his mind, a discordant
repetition. He staggered to a couch and lay down.

Other words began to join the whirlpool of meaning and
implication that was the original message: After six years
. . . the *Hope of Man* . . . after six years, when by even his
minimum estimates he had pictured it a good fifth of the way
to the Centaurus suns . . . re-entering the atmosphere of
Earth.

Lying there, Hewitt thought: "And for ten years I've accepted Astronomer John Lesbee's theory that our sun is due

to show some of the characteristics of a Cepheid Variable—within months now!"

Worse, he had spent the greater part of his huge, inherited fortune to build the giant vessel. The world had ridiculed the West's richest sucker; Joan had left him, taking the children; and only the vast, interstellar colonizing plan had finally won him government support for the journey itself—

All that now was totally nullified by the return of the *Hope of Man*, on the eve of the very disaster it had been built to avoid.

Hewitt thought hopelessly, "What could have made John Lesbee turn back—?"

His bitter reverie ended, as the phone began to ring. He climbed off the couch, and as he went to answer, he thought, "I'll have to go aboard and try to persuade them. As soon as they land, I'll—"

This time, his caller was an official of the Space Patrol. Hewitt listened, trying to grasp the picture the other was presenting. It had proved impossible to communicate with those aboard.

"We've had men in space suits at all the observation ports, Mr. Hewitt, and on the bridge. Naturally, they couldn't see in, since it's one-way-vision material. But they pounded on the metal for well over an hour, and received no response."

Hewitt hesitated. He had no real comment to make, but said finally, "How fast is the ship going?"

"It's overtaking the earth at about a thousand miles an hour."

Hewitt scarcely heard the reply. His mind was working faster now. He said, "I authorize all expense necessary to get inside. I'll be there myself in an hour."

As he headed for his private ship, he was thinking, "If I can get inside, I'll talk to them. I'll convince them. I'll force them to go back."

He felt remorseless. It seemed to him that, for the first time in the history of the human race, any means of compulsion was justified.

Two hours later, he said, "You mean, the airlock won't open?"

He said it incredulously, while standing inside the rescue ship, *Molly D*, watching a huge magnet try to unscrew one of the hatches of the *Hope of Man*. Reluctantly, Hewitt drew his restless mind from his own private purposes.

He felt impatient, unwilling to accept the need to adjust to the possibility that there had been trouble aboard. He said urgently, "Keep trying! It's obviously stuck. That lock was made to open easily and quickly."

He was aware that the others had let him take control of rescue operations. In a way, it was natural enough. The *Molly D* was a commercial salvage vessel, which had been commandeered by the Space Patrol. Now that Hewitt was aboard, the representative of the patrol, Lieutenant Commander Mardonell, had assumed the role of observer. And the permanent captain of the vessel took instructions, as a matter of course, from the man paying the bills.

More than an hour later, the giant magnet had turned the round lock-door just a little over one foot. Pale, tense, and astounded, Hewitt held counsel with the two officers.

The altimeter of the *Molly D* showed ninety-one miles. Lieutenant Commander Mardonell made the decisive comment about that: "We've come down about nine miles in sixty-eight minutes. Since we're going forward as well as down, we'll strike the surface on a slant in ten hours."

It was evident that it would take much longer than that to unscrew the thirty-five feet of thread on the lock-door, at one foot per hour.

Hewitt considered the situation angrily. He still thought of this whole boarding problem as a minor affair, an irritation. "We'll have to burn in or use a big drill," he said. "Cut through the wall."

He radioed for one to be sent ahead. But even with the full authority of the Space Patrol behind him, two and a half hours went by before it was in position. Hewitt gave the order to start the powerful drill motor. He left instructions: "Call me when we're about to penetrate."

He had been progressively aware of exhaustion, as much mental as physical. He retreated to one of the ship's bunks and lay down.

He slept tensely, expecting to be called any moment. He turned and twisted, and, during his wakeful periods, his mind was wholly on the problem of what he would do when he got inside the ship.

He awoke suddenly and saw by his watch that more than five hours had gone by. He dressed with a sense of disaster. He was met by Mardonell. The Space Patrol officer said, "I didn't call you, Mr. Hewitt, because when it became apparent that we weren't going to get it, I contacted my headquarters. As a result we've been getting advice from some of the world's greatest scientists." The man was quite pale, as he finished. "I'm afraid it's no use. All the advice in the world hasn't helped that drill, and cutting torches did no good."

"What do you mean?"

"Better go take a look."

The drill was still turning as Hewitt approached. He ordered it shut off, and examined the metal wall of the *Hope of Man*. It had been penetrated—he measured it—to a depth of three quarters of a millimeter.

"But that's ridiculous," Hewitt protested. "That metal drilled easily enough six years ago when the ship was built."

Mardonell said, "We've had two extra drills brought up. Diamonds don't mean a thing to that metal." He added, "It's been calculated that she'll crash somewhere in the higher foothills of the Rockies. We've been able to pin it down pretty accurately, and people have been warned."

Hewitt said, "What about those aboard? What about—" He stopped. He had been intending to ask, "What about the human race?" He didn't say it. That was a special madness of his own, which would only irritate other people.

Trembling, he walked over to a porthole of the rescue ship. He guessed they were about fifteen miles above the surface of Earth. Less than two hours before crashing.

When that time limit had dwindled to twenty minutes, Hewitt gave the order to cast off. The rescue ship withdrew slowly from the bigger host, climbing as she went. A little later, Hewitt stood watching with an awful, empty feeling, as the huge round ship made its first contact with Earth below, the side of a hill.

At just under a thousand miles an hour, horizontal velocity, it plowed through the soil, creating a cloud of dust. From where Hewitt and his men watched, no sound was audible, but the impact must have been terrific.

"That did it," said Hewitt, swallowing. "If anybody was alive aboard, they died at that moment."

It needed no imagination to picture the colossal concussion. All human beings inside would now be bloody splotches against a floor, ceiling, or wall.

A moment later, the sound of the impact reached him. It arrived with all the power and sharpness of a sonic boom, and the salvage vessel itself shuddered with its blow. The noise was louder by far than he had anticipated.

Somebody shouted, "She's through the hill!"

Hewitt said, "My God!"

The small mountain, made of rock and packed soil, thicker than a score of ships like the *Hope of Man*, was sheared in two. Through a cloud of dust, Hewitt made out the round ship skimming the high valley beyond. She struck the valley floor, and once again, there was dust. The machine did not slow; showed no reaction to the impact.

It continued at undiminished speed on into the earth.

The dust cleared slowly. There was a hole, over twelve hundred feet in diameter, slanting into the far hillside. The hole began to collapse. Tons of rock crashed down from the upper lip of the cave.

The rescue ship had sunk to a point nearer the ground, and Hewitt heard plainly the thunder of the falling debris.

Rock and soil were still falling when a radio report arrived. A mountain had collapsed fifty miles away. There was a new valley, and somebody had been killed. Three small earthquakes had shaken the neighborhood.

For twenty minutes, the reports piled up. The land was uneasy. Fourteen more earthquakes were recorded. Two of them were the most violent ever recorded in the affected areas. Great fissures had appeared. The ground jumped and trembled. The last temblor had occurred four hundred miles from the first; and they all lined up with the course of the *Hope of Man*.

Abruptly, there came an electrifying message. The round ship had emerged in the desert, and was beginning to climb upward on a long, swift shallow slant.

Less than three hours later, the salvage ship was again clinging to the side of the larger machine. Its huge magnets twisted stubbornly at the great lock-door. To the half-dozen government scientists who had come aboard, Hewitt said, "It took an hour to turn it one foot. It shouldn't take more than thirty-five hours to turn it thirty-five feet. Then, of course, we have the inner door, but that's a different problem." He broke off. "Gentlemen, shall we discuss the fantastic thing that has happened?"

The discussion that followed arrived at no conclusion.

Hewitt said, "That does it!" The outer door had been open for some while, and now, through the thick asbesglas, they

watched the huge magnet make its final turn on the inner
door. As they waited behind the transparent barrier, a thick
metal arm was poked into the airlock, and shoved at the
door. After straining with it for several seconds, its operator
turned and glanced at Hewitt. The latter turned on his
walkie-talkie.

"Come on back inside the ship. We'll put some air pressure
in there. That'll open the door."

He had to fight to keep his anger out of his voice. The
outer door had opened without trouble, once all the turns had
been made. There seemed no reason why the inner door
should not respond in the same way. The *Hope of Man* was
persisting in being recalcitrant.

The captain of the salvage vessel looked doubtful when
Hewitt transmitted the order to him. "If she's stuck," he ob-
jected, "you never can tell just how much pressure it'll take
to open her. Don't forget we're holding two ships together
with magnets. It wouldn't take much to push them apart."

Hewitt frowned over that. He said finally, "Maybe it won't
take a great deal. And if we do get pushed apart, well, we'll
just have to add more magnets." He added swiftly, "Or
maybe we can build a bulkhead into the lock itself, join the
two ships with a steel framework."

It was decided to try a gradual increase in air pressure.
Presently, Hewitt watched the pressure gauge as it slowly
crept up. It registered in pounds and atmospheres. At a fraction over ninety-one atmospheres, the pressure started rapidly
down. It went down to eighty-six in a few seconds, then
steadied, and began to creep up again. The captain barked an
order to the engine room, and the gauge stopped rising. The
man turned to Hewitt.

"Well, that's it. At ninety-one atmospheres, the rubber lin-
ing began to lose air, and didn't seal up again till the pressure
went down."

Hewitt shook his head in bewilderment. "I don't understand it," he said. "That's over twelve hundred pounds to the
square inch."

Reluctantly, he radioed for the equipment that would be
needed to brace the two ships together. While they waited,
they tried several methods of using machinery to push open
the door. None of the methods worked. It was evident that
far higher pressures would be needed to force an entrance.

It required a pressure of nine hundred and seventy-four atmospheres.

The door swung open grudgingly. Hewitt watched the air gauge, and waited for the needle to race downward. The air should be rushing through the open door, on into the ship, dissipating its terrific pressure in the enormous cubic area of the bigger machine. It could sweep through like a tornado, destroying everything it its path.

The pressure went down to nine hundred and seventy-three. There it stopped. There it stayed. Beside Hewitt, a government scientist said in a strangled tone, "But what's happened? It seems to be equalized at an impossible level. How can that be? That's over thirteen thousand pounds to the square inch."

Hewitt drew away from the asbesglas barrier. "I'll have to get a specially designed suit," he said. "Nothing we have would hold that pressure for an instant."

It meant going down to Earth. Not that it would take a great deal of time. There were firms capable of building such a suit in a few days. But he would have to be present in person to supervise its construction. As he headed for a landing craft, Hewitt thought: "All I've got to do is to get aboard, and start the ship back to Centaurus. I'll probably have to go along. But that's immaterial now." It was too late to build more colonizing ships.

He was suddenly confident that the entire unusual affair would be resolved swiftly. He had no premonition.

It was morning at the steel city when he landed. The news of his coming had preceded him; and when he emerged from the space-suit factory shortly after noon, a group of reporters were waiting for him. Hewitt told them what he knew, but left them dissatisfied.

Back at his office, he made a mistake. He called Joan. It was years since they had talked and evidently she was no longer so tense, for she actually came to the phone. Her manner was light. "And what's on *your* mind?" she asked.

"Reconciliation."

"For Pete's sake!" she said, and laughed.

Her voice sounded more strident than when he had last seen her. It struck Hewitt with a pang that the vague reports he had heard, that she was associating not only with one man—which would be normal and to be expected—but with many, were true.

The realization stopped him a little but only a little. He said soberly, "I don't know why that amuses you. What's happened to the profound and undying love which you used to swear would last for all eternity?"

There was a pause, then: "You know," she said, "I really do believe you are simpleton enough, and that you are calling for a reconciliation. But I'm smart these days, and so I'll just put two and two together and guess that the return of your silly ship is probably connected with this call. Do you want me to get the family together and we all go back with you to Centaurus?"

Hewitt had the feeling that, after such an unfruitful beginning, it would be a mistake to continue the conversation. But he persisted anyway. "Why not let me have the children?" he urged. "The trip won't hurt them and at least they'll be out of the way when—"

Joan cut him off at that point. "You see," she laughed, "I figured the whole crazy thing correctly."

With that, she banged the receiver in his ear.

The evening papers phoned him about it, and then carried a garbled account of her version of his proposal to her. In print, the reference to himself as the "baby Nova man" made him cringe. Hewitt hid from reporters who thereafter maintained a twenty-four-hour vigil in the lobby of the hotel where he lived.

Two days later, he needed a police escort to take him to the factory to pick up the specially built tank suit, and then on to the field, where he took off once more for the *Molly D.*

Once there, more than an hour was spent in testing. But at last a magnet drew shut the inner door of the *Hope of Man*. Then the air pressure in the connecting bulkhead was reduced to one atmosphere. Hewitt, arrayed in his new, motor-driven capsule on wheels, was then lifted out of the salvage ship into the bulkhead by a crane. The door locked tight behind him. Air was again pumped into the space. Hewitt watched the suit's air-pressure gauges carefully as the outside pressure was gradually increased to nine hundred and seventy-three atmospheres. When, after many minutes, the tank suit still showed no signs of buckling, he edged it forward in low gear and gently pushed open the door of the big ship.

A few moments later he was inside the *Hope of Man*.

23

DARKNESS!

The change had come at the instant he rolled into the ship. The difference was startling. From outside, the corridor had looked bright and normal. He was in a ghastly gray-dark world. Several seconds went by as he peered into the gloom. His eyes became accustomed to the dim lighting effect. Although years had gone by since he had last been aboard, he was now instantly struck by a sense of smallness.

He was in a corridor which he knew pointed into the heart of the ship. It was narrower than he remembered it. Not only a little narrower; a lot. It had been a broad arterial channel, especially constructed for the passage of large equipment. It was not broad any more.

Precisely how long it was, he couldn't see. Originally, it had run the width of the ship, over a thousand feet. He couldn't see that far. Ahead, the corridor faded into impenetrable shadow.

It seemed not to have shrunk in height. It had been thirty feet high and it still looked thirty.

But it was five feet wide instead of forty. And it didn't look as if it had been torn down and rebuilt. It seemed solid and, besides, rebuilding was all but impossible. The steel framework behind the façade of wall was an integral part of the skeleton of the ship.

He had to make up his mind, then, whether he would continue into the ship. And there was no doubt of that. With his purpose he had to.

He paused to close the airlock door. And there he received another shock. The door distorted as it moved. No such effect had been visible from outside. As he swung it shut, its normal width of twelve feet narrowed to four.

The change was so monstrous that perspiration broke out on his face. And the first tremendous realization was in his mind: "But that's the Lorentz-Fitzgerald Contraction Theory effect."

His mind leaped on to an even more staggering thought: "Why, that would mean this ship is traveling at near the speed of light."

He rejected the notion utterly. It seemed a meaningless concept. There must be some other explanation.

Cautiously, he started his machine forward on its rubber wheels. The captain's cabin was his first destination. As he moved ahead, the shadows opened up reluctantly before him. Not till he was ten feet from it was he able to see the ramp that led up to the next level.

The reappearance of things remembered relieved him. What was more important, they seemed to be at about the right distance. First, the airlock, then the ramp, and then many workshops. The corridor opened out at the ramp, then narrowed again. Everything looked eerily cramped because of the abnormal narrowing effect. But the length seemed to be right.

He expected the door of the captain's cabin to be too narrow for his space suit to get into. However, as he came up to it, he saw that its width was as he remembered it. Hewitt nodded to himself, thought, "Of course, even by the Lorentz-Fitzgerald theory, that would be true. Contraction would be in the direction of flight." Since the door was at right angles to the flight line, the size of the doorway was not affected. The doorjamb, however, would probably be narrower.

The jamb *was* narrower. Hewitt had stopped his suit to stare at it. Now, he felt himself pale with tension. "It doesn't fit," he told himself. "Like the hall, it's narrower only by a factor of eight, whereas the air pressure varies 973 to one.

Once more he assured himself that the explanation could not possibly include the famous contraction theory. Speed was, after all, not an aspect of this situation. The *Hope of Man* was practically at rest, whatever its velocity might have been in the past.

He stopped that thought with: "I'm wasting time! I've got to get going!"

Acutely conscious again that this was supposed to be a quick, exploratory journey, he shifted the softly spinning motor into gear, and moved forward through the doorway.

The outer room of the captain's apartment was empty. Hewitt rolled forward into the beautiful suite and headed for the master bedroom. Its door was closed but it opened at the touch of one of his power-driven appendages. He entered with embarrassed hesitation; he had a typical attitude about intruding on people in bed. The room held twin beds. A woman lay in the nearer one, but she was covered by a thin sheet and so he could see only a part of one arm and shoulder and her head. She was turned away from him. At first glance, she seemed normal enough and one glance was all he gave her, for at that moment his gaze was caught by the man.

He was curled up against the headboard in a twisted position—the position a man might be in who had been flung out of control by a sudden stop or start. Parts of his body were narrow and other parts were not, an anomaly that seemed to derive from the curled-up state. Hewitt rolled around the bed for another view. Seen from the front, the man looked normal.

But, from the side, his head and body looked like a caricature of a human being, such as might be seen in a badly distorted circus mirror.

Hewitt could not recall ever having seen the fellow before. Certainly, he bore no resemblance to Captain John Lesbee, who had commanded the great vessel on its departure six years earlier.

Then and there, Hewitt suspended his judgment. Some of the phenomena suggested the Lorentz-Fitzgerald effect. But most of what he had seen could only be explained if the ship were traveling simultaneously at several different speeds. Impossible.

Hewitt began his retreat from the captain's cabin. His mind was almost blank but he paused long enough to glance in to the other bedroom. There were three beds, each with a young woman in it. They also were covered by thin bedding, but what he could see of them was distorted. He drew back, shuddering. Physiological caricature looked worse on a woman, or so it seemed.

As he emerged onto the corridor again, Hewitt consciously braced himself, consciously accepted the abnormality of his environment. As he raced along in his thick, tanklike suit, he grew more observant and more thoughtful, more willing to see what there was to look at. He began to peer into the apartments that had been built for the ship's officers and for the scientists. In almost every instance the master bedroom was occupied by a woman and the lesser bedrooms by children.

When he saw his first teen-ager, Hewitt lifted the bedsheet from him entirely—it required a very considerable power to do so—and stared down at the distorted body. He wanted to make sure that it was actually a youth. It was. Despite the caricature, there was no doubt. He saw several more after that, and girls as well as boys, some of whom seemed as much as eighteen years old.

But where were the men?

He found, first, three rather rough-looking fellows in apartments along a second corridor, near the captain's cabin. They also were in bed, and since they did not all face in the direction of flight, they presented an amazing assortment. When he lifted the bedsheets from the first man, Hewitt saw a body that was, literally, as thin as a post, gaunt and incredible. The second man was foreshortened. He simply looked crippled, stunted. The third one was narrow through the thickness of the body, a mere sliver of a man, like a silhouette.

Except for these three, he saw no other men until he came to the large semidormitories on the lower decks. Here, in the small bedrooms that led off the large lounges, he found what he estimated were several hundred men. No women were among them, which was puzzling. There seemed to be no reason for having the men down here and the women and children on the upper floors.

Hewitt was bemused now. As he headed for the engine room, it was apparent to him that this ship had aboard it men, women, and children of all ages, and that he knew not a single one of them. He who had met all of the colonists, technical people, scientists, women, however fleetingly in some instances, recognized not one person.

Hewitt reached the engine room. His first glance at the line of meters shocked him.

The pile was as hot as a hundred hells. The transformer output meter needle was amazingly steady for the colossal load it was bearing. And the resistance to acceleration must be tremendous, for the accelerometer essentially registered zero. As he studied the instruments, Hewitt found himself remembering his conversation with Tellier about attempting to reach the speed of light. Suddenly, he frowned. The figure he was getting from the velocity integrator was surely wrong: 198,700. . . . *Faster than light!*

Hewitt thought, "But surely that doesn't mean it still—"
His mind refused to hold the thought. Right there he began his retreat, back to the airlock and the *Molly D*.

24

During Hewitt's absence from the salvage vessel, a great man had come aboard. He listened with the others to Hewitt's account, and then remained silent and thoughtful through most of the discussion that followed. His presence had a subduing effect on the younger government scientists aboard. No one had very much to say. The attitude seemed to be: "You stick your neck out first!"

As a result, the conversation remained "close to the ground." Phrases like "a natural explanation" abounded. When he had listened to all he could stand, Hewitt said impatiently, "After all, these things *have* happened. What do we mean by natural?"

He was about to say more, when the great man cleared his throat and spoke for the first time since he had been introduced. "Gentlemen, I should like to try to clear away the debris that has accumulated at the beginning of this obstacle course."

He turned to Hewitt. "I want to congratulate you, sir. For the first time in history, the mythical observer—that mathematical oddity—has come to life. You have seen phenomena that, till now, have never been more than a set of equations."

Without any further preliminary, he laughed into an explanation for what had happened, in which he accepted that "aspects of speed of light are involved." He continued, "At this stage we need not concern ourselves with how this can possibly be, though speculations are unquestionably in order. I toss in one of my own. Mr. Hewitt saw that the velocitors showed a speed of more than light-speed. Is it possible that in attaining such a speed, the ship is confronting us with a true condition of space and matter which has hitherto been hidden from us? I speculate that the ship is traveling at more than light-speed in its own zone of existence, in a sort of parallel time to now, this minute, this second."

Further knowledge of the event was of course needed. But it could wait. He went on, "The time has come for a practical solution. I offer the following."

Copies of a carefully written letter must be placed in the hands of various key personnel on the ship, for them to read when they awakened.

In the letter the circumstances would be described, and those in charge would be urged to cut off both the drive and the robot pilot. If this were not done within a certain period—taking into account the difference in time rate—it would be assumed that the letter had been misunderstood. At this point Hewitt would go aboard, attempt to shut off the robot, and reverse the drive personally.

However, before leaving the ship after delivering the letter, Hewitt should set off a general alarm aboard to ensure that the awakening took place quickly.

Hewitt frowned over the suggestion. He could think of no logical reason why it shouldn't work. And yet, having been aboard that foreshortened, eerie vessel, with its nuclear piles operating to the very limit of safety and its lopsided passengers moveless as in death, he had a feeling that some factor was being neglected.

He found himself remembering the man crumpled against the headboard of the bed in the captain's cabin. Such an incongruity needed to be explained. But the older man's words had also brought several thoughts of a practical nature. His tank suit needed to be modified and equipped with power tools to set off the alarm, and to perform labors that would be necessary within the frame of such a time difference. And, as for making a third trip later on, he said slowly, "If it turns out that I have to shut off the drives also, then I'll have to take along food and water. The time difference could make such a task very involved."

It had required thirty-five hours to open an airlock, which normally took five minutes. By comparison, reversing the drive might involve weeks of not necessarily hard but certainly persistent labor. It would be better if those aboard could do it.

Another scientist suggested that the suit might also be fitted with instruments for detecting and observing and recording the drive states connected with light-speed phenomena.

This thought, unleashed a tornado of excited, creative ideas, which Hewitt finally stopped with the statement: "Now, look, gentlemen, only so much additional equipment can be added to this suit. So why don't a couple of you come down with me to the factory, and you can work with them to add the possible modifications? Meanwhile, the letter can be written and copies made. We should be back here reasonably soon, and then I'll go aboard again."

This was agreed on, and they took the suit back to the factory. Hewitt left the scientists there to see that the job was done right and he went outside.

He had estimated that it would require a week to do all that had to be done. He proposed to spend the first few hours of that time in sleep.

He headed straight for his hotel room.

25

Aboard the ship, Lesbee V awakened.

He lay quite still, momentarily not remembering what had happened, simply lying there in the darkness like a child, not thinking.

Then memory rushed in on him. He thought, "Oh, my God!"

For many seconds he felt scared, but suddenly relief came. For he was still alive. Translight-speed was not lethal. The feared instant when the ship was traveling exactly at the speed of light had arrived, been experienced, and was behind them.

Lying there, he wondered how long he had been blacked out. That thought brought a new sense of urgency, the realization that he should be down in the engine room, testing, checking, preparing for the slowdown.

He thought of Gourdy. "Can he be dead?". he wondered hopefully.

He reached up and turned on the light beside the bunk. It was an automatic action, and it was only as the light flooded his little prison cell that he realized that electric impulses and light waves and antigravity seemed to be functioning as normally as ever.

. . . Wonder came. Yet that fitted the theory that at light-speed, light still traveled at the speed of light.

Lesbee freed himself from his acceleration belt and sat up.

He heard a noise outside his cell. A key sounded in a lock. The door beyond the metal bars swung open. Gourdy, wearing a bandage on his head, peered in at him. Behind the captain, loomed the larger figure of a former kitchen worker named Harcourt.

As he saw Gourdy, instant disappointment hit Lesbee. He had expected it; his analysis about it was correct; but somehow the reality—that Gourdy had not been fatally injured—violated a basic hope that he had cherished. . . . As quickly as it had come, the disappointment faded.

He remembered that Gourdy's coming here was victory.

Lesbee's spirit lifted. It was true. This was why he had programmed the drives: to force this shrewd, murderous little man to come to him for help.

He spoke quickly, to get in the first word, to guide the thought. "I was knocked unconscious. I just came to. What happened? Is everybody safe?"

He saw that Gourdy was staring at him with a baffled expression. "You were caught, too!" the man said.

Lesbee merely stared at him. He had a fear of overdramatizing, was convinced that even a single repetition might be a giveaway.

"Lesbee, you're sure this is not part of some scheme?"

Lesbee was able to say that there was no scheme, and it was true, in that his plan had not carried him beyond this moment. Therefore, the scheme such as it was, was already a thing of the past. From this instant, he and everyone aboard confronted a situation new to man: the phenomena related to supralight-speed.

The denial must have reassured Gourdy. He hesitated, but only for a moment. Then, roughly: "I'm going to take one more chance on you, Lesbee, so you get down to the engine room! Harcourt'll go with you—and take care! No funny stuff!"

Gourdy must have realized the futility of threats. "Look, Lesbee," he pleaded, "find out what happened, straighten it out—and we'll talk. O.K.?"

Lesbee did not trust him; could not. He recognized that Gourdy's situation had not changed, that the new captain still must not go to Earth. But aloud he said, "O.K. Of course."

Gourdy managed a facial contortion that was meant to be a friendly smile. "I'll see you later," he said.

He departed to interrogate the other prisoners. At this moment, having cleared Lesbee—in his own mind—his suspicion had turned on Miller. Who else could have done it but the only other man who had been in the engine room? He recalled how Miller had examined some of the dials, touched them. That was when it must have happened, Gourdy decided savagely. "Right there in front of my eyes!" The mere thought enraged him.

Lesbee, with Harcourt trailing him, reached the alternate control room. A quick glance into the viewplates indicated that there was plenty of balck space ahead. Quickly, trembling a little in his haste, he programmed the drives for reverse on a twelve g plus eleven artificial-gravity basis. The programming done, he reached for the master switch, grasped it—

And then he stopped.

It seemed to him, in this moment of ultimate decision, that he had several vital things to consider.

The acceleration to translight-speeds had achieved the purpose that he had vaguely anticipated. It had freed him from prison. But it had changed nothing basic in his situation.

No matter what he did, if he failed, or even if he merely failed to act, he was slated to be murdered. That was his certainty, and it must govern what he did now.

. . . Get Harcourt's gun, and incapacitate the man, somehow, in the process; bind him, hold him, even kill him—if absolutely necessary. But, whatever, put him out of action.

Then rescue Tellier . . . and the two of them get off the ship exactly as they had planned it.

The decisions made, once more he started to reach for the switch.

But this time he drew back without touching it. There was another factor to consider, less personal, perhaps even more important. He thought, "Why did I black out at the transition point? That should be explained."

People were hard to knock out. That had been discovered many times aboard the big ship. Short of being given an anesthetic, people clung to consciousness under conditions of extreme shock and pain with a tenacity that was almost incredible.

Lesbee half-turned to the big man, asked, "Did you become unconscious, Harcourt?"

"Yeah."

"Do you remember anything about it?"

"Nope. Just conked out. Came to. Thought to myself: 'Boy, I'd better get up to Gourdy!' Found him piled up against the headboard of his bed and—"

Lesbee interrupted. "No thoughts?" he asked. "No pictures, no dreams, no odd memories? Just before consciousness, I mean."

He himself had had only some vague fantasies and memory images in reverse.

"Well-l-l!" Harcourt sounded doubtful. "Come to think of it, I did have a dream. Kind of vague now."

Lesbee waited. The expression on the man's fleshy face indicated that he seemed to be straining for the memory, and so there was no point in urging him.

Harcourt said, "You know, Mr. Lesbee, when it comes right down to it, I guess we human beings have really got truth in us."

Lesbee groaned inwardly. This man was too slow in thought and tongue. He said hurriedly, "I'd better reverse the engine, Harcourt. We can talk later."

Once more he took hold of the relay. This time he gently closed the switch. The job done, Lesbee seated himself in the master chair, picked up an attached microphone, and spoke into the ship's loud-speaker system, announcing that deceleration would begin in less than a minute. Having done this, Lesbee was about to strap himself into his chair when he glanced at Harcourt and saw that the man had already fastened his belt.

The observation electrified him. Should he attack the other man now?

Breathless, Lesbee sank back into his own chair. "Not now!" he thought. There were too many unknowns. Now, if there was a struggle, it could be interrupted by the deceleration. "Wait!" Lesbee thought. With trembling fingers, he fastened his own belt.

Uneasily, a little wide-eyed, he watched the dials on the control board.

Abruptly, the needles surged.

Involuntarily, he braced himself. But nothing special happened. He had set up a gap of one g between deceleration thrust and artificial gravity, and that was what it was.

He thought, "Can we depend on that, even at speeds above light?"

The needles continued to show response as before.

Harcourt spoke. "You know, Mr. Lesbee, that dream was sure funny. I actually had the picture of every part of my body doing some kind of a flip-flop. I was as big as all space and I could see my insides and all those little, fuzzy, spinning flecks of light, only they weren't small any more, and every single one of 'em stopped spinning and started up in the opposite direction. There was a funny feeling of going backwards. I guess right there is where I blacked out."

Lesbee had turned as the man was describing his subjective experience. Listening, it seemed to him that he was hearing what a simple, uncluttered mind had observed with a pure inner vision.

"... *flip-flop.* ..." What else?

"... *as big as all space.* ..." That was the theory: at light-speed, mass became infinite, though size reduced to zero.

"... *fuzzy flecks.* ..." Electrons, for heaven's sake, whirling in their orbits, suddenly reversing—

Of course. Fantastic, but of course.

And, naturally, that *was* where the blackout would occur. Exactly at the moment of reversal. The very structure of life and matter must have been wrenched. He felt a sudden awe, thought, "While we were having these petty squabbles, could it be that the ship was breaking the barriers of time and space?"

He visualized fantasia: the colossal night out there conquered by discovery and utilization of the rules inherent in its structure. Distance defeated totally, even time probably distorted.

Tensely, Lesbee sat, waiting for the ship to cross light-speed, slowing down. Waited for the shock of return to normalcy—

The swift seconds sped by. The needles continued their surging.

Nothing.

26

On Earth, three weeks had gone by.

A disconcerted Hewitt had tried to speed up the various things that had to be accomplished. What money could do, he was able to do. But the human factor would not move a single hour or day faster than its normal rate.

The letter was one of the holdups. Hewitt had it written quickly, and then he dispatched copies of it by special messenger to the various persons who must approve it and sign it.

What with suggested changes and unexplained delays, and the final version being "lost" for a week in the office of the Minister of State, the time dragged on.

But finally, the twelve copies of the letter were in Hewitt's possession, needing only his signature. In its final version, the letter read:

Attention: Aboard the *Hope of Man*

Your ship, the *Hope of Man*, has arrived in the solar system in what seems to be a unique matter-state. The proof of this is the fact that Averill Hewitt, the ship's owner, has twice been aboard and passed among you unseen. In relation to him, all of you aboard the ship had the appearance of suspended animation. The effect is as if the ship is traveling at, or even beyond, the speed of light.

The explanation for this remarkable complexity of behavior is a matter of controversy among Earth scientists, but there is complete agreement on the solution.

Decelerate immediately and as rapidly as possible to minimize the translight-speed effects.

Then attempt radio contact with Earth!

Since the Lorentz-Fitzgerald Contraction Theory may be applicable, it is possible there has been a time as well as a space distortion. Be advised therefore that, on Earth, six years have gone by since the *Hope of Man* set out for Centaurus. This will give you the relevant data by which to evaluate your situation.

Please act at once, since your vessel seems to be homed-in
on Earth and may strike the planet head on if it continues
on its present course.

Most urgently . . .

The first signature space was for Hewitt. The other signato-
ries had graciously left the top line for him. The Minister of
State of the Combined Western Powers had signed immediately below. And below that was the name of the Officer
Commanding Space Fleets (OFCOMSPAF). Then came the
signatures of three scientists: the "great man" physicist—Peter Linden—a leading astronomer, and the head of the government science bureau.

A variety of officials and professional observers accompanied Hewitt aboard the *Molly D:* Space Patrol officers, a
doctor, a member of the cabinet, a representative from the
Asiatic Powers, and several space physicists. . . .

The *Hope of Man*, as was to be expected, had outdistanced
Earth, in the course of the three weeks, by over five hundred
thousand miles. But, more important, since it was not affected
by the sun's gravity, the solar system's over-all twelve-miles-
per-second motion, in the direction of Aries, had caused the
ship to have an apparent drift at that speed diagonally past
the sun, a total of ten million miles. Twice during this time,
the big ship had been observed to adjust course in such a
manner that it would intercept Earth's orbit at some later
time.

This was believed to be an indication that the ship's sen-
sor-guidance equipment was still programmed to zero in on
Earth.

Urgently, Hewitt ordered the takeoff.

Eight days later, the salvage vessel again attached itself to
the huge ship. That was nearly a month, Earth time, since its
previous journey. . . . But it would be about half an hour on
the *Hope of Man*—

As soon as the airlock was open and connected, Hewitt
guided his tank suit into it. He went straight to the captain's
cabin—and ran into his first problem. The black-haired man
who had been so dramatically crumpled against the headboard of one of the beds in the master bedroom—was gone.
The woman was still in the next bed.

Hewitt peered uncertainly into the gloom of the adjoining
bedroom, and there also—each in a separate bed—were the

three other women. But the person with whom he had planned to leave one of the letters, was nowhere to be found in the apartment.

Not that it mattered. It had been generally agreed by the experts on the *Molly D* that a total of twelve letters placed with different persons throughout the ship would effectively spread the news.

Hewitt left a copy on the man's unmade bed, several copies with women in the officers' cabins, four copies with men selected at random from the two hundred in the dormitory in the lower section of the ship, and a copy each with two men whom he found seated in adjoining chairs in the engine room, strapped in by safety belts.

Hewitt had come to the engine room last because he had photographic equipment attached to his suit, with which he had been requested to take a series of pictures showing the positions of all the dials. The physicists on the *Molly D* were particularly anxious for an opportunity to make a complete correlation.

He took the pictures. It was when he pressed the button that automatically folded the camera back into its protective case that Hewitt had a sudden thought. Those speed dials! They were different from what they had been on his previous visit.

His gaze flashed over to the velocity meters again. There was a red line on the meter, indicating light-speed, and the needle which last time had been far over the line, now hovered on the red.

Hewitt felt an intense, horrifying shock of fear.

The ship was already programmed for slowing down. And, in slowing, it had already reduced speed to within a few miles above the speed of light.

He took it for granted that the moment of transition would be dangerous for him. He was heading frantically out of the engine room by the time that thought was completed. The people aboard had survived crossing the line in the other direction. But they were a part of the speed process. How would the changeover, in reverse, affect someone who was not involved in the contraction? One thing seemed certain: Even at 973 to one, in his favor, there was not enough time to cover the distance he had to go.

It was as he was turning a corner, from which he could actually see—dimly—the distant airlock, that he felt his first nausea. He had no idea what might happen. But it occurred to him that he should slow down.

He applied the brake. He was aware of the tank suit rolling to a stop. And then—

Something grabbed his body behind and squeezed it mercilessly. The sensation of being caught by a gaint hand was so realistic that he squirmed to release himself from its clutch.

The great hand began to slip. He had the feeling then of being squirted from a space that was too small for him, into something—vast.

That was the last thing he remembered as blackness closed over him.

27

Something hit Lesbee.

It hit him deep inside first, then not so deep, then all over.

The progression from impact to anguish to agony to unbearable pain was rapid. But he felt every excruciating moment of it.

He must have been in a dreamlike state—though this time he had no fantasies—because he came to suddenly, with the realization that the ship had made the transition. And from the feel of deceleration, they were continuing to slow down.

Trembling, Lesbee thought, "We made it!"

. . . Beyond light-speed and back again! Out of normal space time and return.

Without looking down, Lesbee unfastened his belt and stood up. He was so intent on the bank of instruments, that Hewitt's letter fell from his lap, unnoticed. Utterly fascinated by the drama of the dials, he walked slowly forward.

Behind him, Harcourt said, "Hey, what's this?"

Lesbee glanced around. What he saw made no sense. Harcourt was reading what looked like a letter.

Once more, Lesbee faced about and studied the instrument board.

28

When Hewitt opened his eyes after his blackout, he saw that his tank suit had tilted over against one wall. Exactly how that had come about was not clear.

He had an impression that something else was different—but there was no time to notice what it was.

There was a fear in him that his vehicle might tip. He grabbed hastily at the controls, put on the power, and slowly eased off the brake. The suit rolled closer to the wall, then settled back on all four wheels.

Hewitt breathed easier, thought, "We must have crossed light-speed without too much problem. It was pretty painful, but it apparently didn't do me any harm."

The thought ended. He felt his eyes grow large and round. He gazed wildly at the corridor. It was brightly lighted. The dim, eerie, shadowy effect was gone as if it had never been. He noticed something else. The corridor was not narrow any more. He couldn't tell exactly, but he estimated that it was back to its full width, as it had originally been constructed. Then and there the truth dawned on Hewitt.

He was no longer an observer of this scene. He was part of it. He also would now appear lopsided to another person coming aboard from the *Molly D.* To himself, and to those aboard the ship, he would be quite normal. People affected by the Lorentz-Fitzgerald phenomenon were not aware of any difference in themselves. The contraction affected their bodies as well as their frame of reference. Nothing was actually distorted with respect to it.

Hewitt remembered the sensation of being squeezed. Readjustments within his body, he analyzed, were unevenly distributed during the change. His front changing faster than his back.

The memory of the pain was suddenly sharper. He shuddered.

Then he thought: "I wonder where we are."

A minute or two had gone by on the *Hope of Man*, since his return to consciousness. On the *Molly D*, that alone was sixteen to thirty hours. But Hewitt knew that the contraction phenomenon at light-speed might have a few more surprises for him.

Years may have whisked by outside.

If that were true, then the *Hope of Man* might, by this time, have proceeded light-years from the solar system.

Hewitt grew calm and cool and grim. It occurred to him that he had accidentally achieved the position he had wanted to be in ever since he was first informed of the ship's return.

From the beginning, his purpose had been to get aboard and persuade a shipload of people to start again on the long journey to the Centaurus suns.

Or, if persuasion failed, to force them. Or trick them—

It felt a little odd; he had a peculiar empty sense that he did not have enough control of this situation. But here he was.

On the wall beside Hewitt, a man's voice said from a loudspeaker: "Attention, everyone! This is Captain Gourdy. I have just been informed by Mr. Lesbee from the engine room, that deceleration will continue at one g until further notice. You may remove your safety belts."

Incredibly, tears started to Hewitt's eyes. He realized almost immediately what it was. After all the strangeness, now suddenly there was the sound of a human voice. More important, it gave a normal message and it mentioned a familiar name.

"*. . . Mr. Lesbee from the engine room. . . .*"

Lesbee! . . . Hewitt recalled the two men who had been in the engine room—each had looked at least thirty. It provided another perspective on the time that had elapsed since the round ship's original departure from Earth.

What was more important, the words identified, and located, a specific person to whom he might talk. Hewitt felt an intense excitement. Eagerly, he turned his machine around and headed back toward the engine room, from which he had fled only—minutes—ago.

A few moments later, he rounded a corner—and brought his mobile suit to an abrupt halt.

For a man was in the act of emerging from one of the middle-level cabins. He stepped out into the corridor, closed the door behind him, and then turned. He saw Hewitt.

It must have been an instantaneous strange sight for him. He stiffened. Hewitt rolled his machine forward, and said through his speaker, "Don't be afraid!"

The man simply stood there, a blank look on his face.

Hewitt said, "While your ship was traveling faster than light, it passed through the solar system. I was put aboard from an Earth warship. I'm the owner of the *Hope of Man*. My name is Averill Hewitt."

His statement was not factual in all details. But it was what he would have liked to be true, particularly the part about the warship, with its implication of powerful forces standing by.

If the man heard him, it did not show. There was a blank look in his eyes, a paleness in his thin cheeks.

Hewitt said gently, "What's your name?"

No answer.

Hewitt recognized shock when he saw it. "Hey," he said sharply. "Snap out of it! What's your name?"

The sharp, penetrating tones did the job. "Earth," the man croaked. "You're from Earth!"

"I was put aboard from an Earth battleship," said Hewitt. "Now, tell me—what's been going on aboard the *Hope of Man?* What *is* going on?"

It was hard to get the information. The man seemed not to grasp how little Hewitt knew. But his name was Lee Winance, and Hewitt learned from him a part of the ship's history. About how much time had elapsed. About Lesbee's and then Gourdy's seizure of power. These were recent realities to Winance.

Hewitt was even able to piece together something of the social conditions aboard: the multiwife situation among the officers and—until Gourdy's rebellion—the permanent caste system.

The information made the problem so much more complex that presently Hewitt sat and stared at the man helplessly.

He thought: "Five generations!"

These people were complete strangers to Earth.

As Hewitt sat there, bemused, Winance abruptly darted past him and raced off around the corner and along the corridor from which he had come a few minutes before. Hewitt rolled his machine back and called after the fleeing figure.

"Tell Captain Gourdy I want to see him but that I'm going to the engine room first."

The man did not slow in his headlong flight. And a few moments later, he disappeared around another corner.

In the engine room, Harcourt had already called Gourdy—who had meanwhile returned to the captain's cabin. Gourdy listened to the account with a frown, and stared at the letter that the big man held up for him to see. It seemed to be part of a conspiracy, but its meaning was obscure enough so that he presently said uneasily, "Bring that letter up here right away."

He had not yet gone into his own bedroom and so had not found the copy that had been left for him.

Hewitt, who had resumed his journey to the engine room, arrived there without further incident, and found John Lesbee V alone.

Lesbee caught a glimpse of the intruder from the corner of one eye, and he turned—

After the initial amazement, and wonder, and dawning understanding, the result of that conversation was—Lesbee's normal sense of caution was briefly penetrated, and suspended.

Later, he could only remember one response he made to Hewitt's statements, during those few minutes of excited blurting of his true feelings: ". . . Go back out into space! Never!"

What sobered him finally was the sight of a light flashing on one of the boards. It was a warning-signal device that he had set up. It meant a detector system was spying on him.

Gourdy!

Exactly how long the light had been flickering, Lesbee had no idea. He groaned inwardly with the realization that the one earlier statement he could remember making, would stand against him in the mind of that suspicious little man.

All in an instant, Lesbee was his old self again: the man whose mind could go one step beyond what other devious minds were thinking. Standing there, he made his first attempt to fit Hewitt and Hewitt's background into the cosmos that was the ship.

He thought: "He can't possibly adjust rapidly enough to the murder that's here. So he'll be a pawn."

The question was, how could he use such a powerful pawn for his own purposes?

Lesbee decided that the man was actually, at this stage, a

source of information and a foil in the subtle job of defeating Gourdy.

Hewitt had had his own sobering thoughts. If time slippage into the future had actually occurred, then the disaster to Sol either had or had not happened. They could go to Earth and see if it were damaged and to what extent. Then—and not till then—would it be necessary to decide what to do next.

Whether to land or return to space was not a problem if the decision could be made on the basis of truth.

Greatly relieved, he said firmly, "As owner of the *Hope of Man*, I command you to set course for the solar system and do everything necessary for us to determine the real situation on Earth."

Lesbee said, "I'm sorry, Mr. Hewitt, I'll have to have that as an order from Captain Gourdy. He is in sole command of this ship."

Lesbee felt greatly relieved at having had the chance to say those exact words. Temporarily, at least, they ought to reassure Gourdy.

The objection startled Hewitt. He recognized it as a reasonable statement. But it brought home to him something he had literally not thought of until this instant. Suddenly, he saw that his ownership rights depended on Earth power.

But, according to the dire prediction of which he was a principal advocate, there would by now be no Earth power.

Sitting there, he could feel himself sinking, shrinking, his importance dwindling, his special position becoming meaningless.

Almost as an echo to his thought came Lesbee's voice: "Why don't you go and talk to Captain Gourdy?"

. . . Talk to . . . Gourdy. Try to persuade the powers that be. . . . And be careful. . . ! For it was already obvious that Gourdy had the decision of life or death—

Hewitt was vaguely aware that he had turned his machine and was heading for the door. Outside, in the corridor, he did not turn toward the captain's cabin, but, instead, hurriedly guided his machine to a down ramp, emerging presently on a floor where there were storerooms.

He entered one where there were many pieces of equipment stacked close to the ceiling. Each segment was locked in a cradle or compartment. Hewitt rolled into the shadowy space between two stacks and manipulated the release mechanism of the tank suit.

The rubber separated with a wheezing sound. The two sections of the apparatus were driven apart to the limit of the two bolts that connected them. Hewitt crawled out between the bolts, and a moment later stood on the floor on his own two feet.

He was trembling a little and he felt weak from the very real fear that was in him. But he was, he discovered, strong enough to climb to the top of a compartment near the ceiling. He sank breathlessly down onto the shadowed surface.

He lay there watching the little spy light blinking on the dashboard of his capsule machine. As soon as it ceased, as it did suddenly, he climbed down quickly and drove off as fast as the machine could carry him.

29

When he fled from Hewitt, Lee Winance went straight to Captain Gourdy's apartment, found him there, and told his story of meeting Hewitt.

Gourdy listened with narrowed eyes as the man's improbable story unfolded. A suspicion grew in him that somehow this person—Winance—whom he had always regarded as a nonentity, was involved in a conspiracy.

Swiftly, the absurdity of such an idea struck him.

"Just a minute!" he said peremptorily. "Stay right here!"

He walked to the door leading to the captain's study. The moment he was out of sight, he ran headlong for a small private connecting room where the detector system was located. . . . He focused the scanners on the engine room.

For many seconds he gazed incredulously at the apparition of Hewitt and his mobile capsule, and then, as the import of the conversation between the two men penetrated, he listened with increasing thoughtfulness. When Hewitt hurriedly drove off, Gourdy followed him with his scanners and watched him hide in one of the storerooms. Throughout, the only question in his mind was: "Shall I kill him, or use him?"

He had the abrupt realization that whichever it was would require as a preliminary that he capture the intruder. As he shut off the detector system, intending to return to the outer room, he grew aware that the elder of Captain Browne's two widows had slipped into the room.

"Who is that man?" she asked in amazement.

Her name was Ruth, and she was a patrician-looking woman in her early thirties. He had already developed a strong desire for her, and had restrained himself only because of even stronger political considerations; so now he treated her with the respect of a man who presently hoped to take possession.

He explained about Hewitt but also added that it looked as if Earth had been destroyed, and finished, "Better get everybody up, eat breakfast, and await events. Looks like important decisions will be made shortly."

She nodded and went off. Gourdy joined Winance.

He tossed a spare automatic at the other. Winance caught it awkwardly.

"Come along!" said Gourdy.

He headed for the corridor door.

Winance trailed behind him, pale and breathless. "Where we going, sir?"

"Going to catch that fellow you saw."

"But he's armed."

"So are we."

"Oh!"

Gourdy smiled. The man's reaction reassured him about human nature. Fear still ruled all and, paradoxically, frightened people could still be forced to take risks by someone who was not afraid.

Gourdy said, "You just stand by and do as I say."

"O.K., boss."

As they emerged onto the corridor, Harcourt came into view around a distant bend. Gourdy waited for him, and a minute later the three of them headed for the nearest elevator. In the elevator, Gourdy silently read the letter. It was a confirmation of what he had already seen and convinced him that he had better not do anything hastily.

But his plan to capture Hewitt remained unchanged.

When they came to the storeroom in which Hewitt had taken refuge, it was Gourdy who softly led the way inside.

His strategy was to take up position beside Hewitt's vehicle and from there call for surrender.

And so he had his first shock when he couldn't find the mobile unit. It was an electrifying sensation, like suddenly stepping from something solid into emptiness. The three men spent ten frantic minutes searching the storeroom. But there was no one in it. The conviction that finally came to Gourdy was that he had somehow been outsmarted, but he didn't quite know how.

"Still, he thought, "if we've really slipped into the future, he can't get away."

Another urge had been growing on him. He wanted to get up to the bridge to see if Earth and its sun really were nearby.

That was where he now headed.

30

After Hewitt left the engine room, Lesbee ostensibly returned to his work on the panel he was removing. But his attention was actually on the flickering spy light.

It stopped flashing suddenly.

He waited to make sure. When there was no longer any doubt, he ran for the viewplate that connected with the bridge, turned it on, and looked through it at the solar system.

The sun was a bright star of the first magnitude. He made a computation on the basis of his measurement of its brightness, that it was somewhat less than a hundredth of a light-year away.

Taking into account what Hewitt had said of the motion of the *Hope of Man* through the solar system, Lesbee made various readings on his slide rule, and calculated that the ship had been projected from fifty to one hundred and fifty years into the future.

That was something to know.

It defeated any plan Hewitt might have to assert *his* rights to command the ship.

Lesbee's next act was to tune in on the bridge's radio receivers, which automatically picked up all incoming messages from the surrounding space. Since Gourdy's take-over, no one but Gourdy and himself had had any real opportunity to receive such messages.

The message that came through now was the first Lesbee had heard.

The message began with a simple three-bell signal and was followed by the words:

"Earth calling. Incoming ships use control channel 71.2 meters for initial communication."

Lesbee broke the connection, shut off the engine-room viewer—and ran for the door. He had to take the chance that Gourdy was preoccupied with Hewitt and that accordingly he would not be seen.

Although it was a dangerous thing to do, he used one of the elevators to go up to the bridge.

Arrived there, he opened the radio-receiver panel, reached in, and tore loose the wires that connected the radio with the enormous aerial network that picked up incoming messages from space.

Hastily, Lesbee replaced the panel and raced down to the alternative control room. Still depending on Gourdy being occupied, he used the scanner system of that complete control board to locate the room where Tellier was held prisoner.

Through the scanner, he saw Tellier lying down in one of the bunks. Lesbee called out softly, and Tellier sat up, then came over to the communicator. Lesbee said, "Listen, we're going to have to get off the ship fast at some specific future time."

He explained rapidly what he had done and said that if necessary he would come down and rescue Tellier at the proper time. He finished, "Don't ask any questions. Just tell me—you'll be prepared to come?"

Tellier was properly responsive. "Same old Lesbee," he said admiringly. But there was a strained look on his face as he added, "John, this is going to be a close thing. But yes, I'll take the chance of going on your say-so."

Lesbee broke the connection and once more ran at top

speed along the corridors. Arrived at the engine room, he sank down in a chair for a few minutes to catch his breath. Then he resumed the phony task of fixing the engines.

31

When Hewitt left the storeroom, he headed up to the captain's cabin by way of the ramps.

He came upon the four women cheerfully getting breakfast ready. They turned as he drove in. Four frightened women stared at him.

Hewitt said in his gentle voice, "Don't be alarmed. I've come to talk to Captain Gourdy."

They grew calm as he explained who he was. Also, it was evident that Ruth had already told the others what she had seen in the detector viewplate.

She asked, "Is it true that Earth is destroyed as our husband says?"

Since Hewitt had not discussed that topic with Lesbee, he realized he was listening to Gourdy propaganda. It gave a bitter irony to his present situation on the *Hope of Man*. He had virtually ruined his reputation by predicting grave danger to Earth from a change in the sun. Yet here on the ship it would be to his advantage if that prediction proved untrue.

For reasons of the struggle for control of the ship in which he was now an unwilling participant, he needed these people to believe that Earth and its military might existed. Only thus could he establish his ownership rights.

It suddenly seemed too dangerous a subject to discuss at all.

He said evasively, significantly, "—our husband?"

"Captain Gourdy!" explained the oldest of the four women, who had already introduced herself as Ruth. She continued with pride in her voice, "We are the captain's wives. That is"—she went on carefully—"Ilsa and I were the original wives of the late Captain Browne. Then we became the second and third wives of Mr. Lesbee when he was captain." She pointed at the slim blond woman, whose blue eyes reminded Hewitt a little of Joan. "This is Ann, Mr. Lesbee's first wife. I understand she's to be sent back to him." The blonde shrugged, but said nothing. Ruth next indicated the sullen young brunette beauty at the table. Marianne is Captain Gourdy's first wife. Naturally, Ilsa and I will now be taken over by him."

Hewitt was discreetly silent. But as he glanced from one to the other of the women and saw their agreement with what Ruth had said, he felt an inner excitement of his own.

These women, he realized, amazed, were the male fantasy come alive. Throughout history, men periodically maneuvered the State so skillfully that women were motivated to accept multiple wife roles, at least in connection with the top leaders. A percentage of men dreamed of having a harem of compliant females all in the same household, at peace with each other, free of that jealous madness which men normally found so painfully ever present in women outside of their own fantasies. The desire for many women was probably some deep psychological need, which those who were possessed by it did not even want to have explained.

Hewitt had never had such needs as an adult. So he could look at these women as would a scientist confronted by a phenomenon of nature.

And—just like that—he had an intuition.

"I shall be the captain," he said. "Therefore, you'll be my wives. So, when I call on you later for any kind of help, you give it immediately." He added, "Don't worry, it won't be anything dangerous."

He finished, "And, of course, don't mention to anyone, not even Captain Gourdy, what I've said until I give you permission."

The women were all suddenly white-faced again. Ruth said finally, breathlessly, "You don't understand. A woman does not choose among men or do anything at all that would indicate that she favors one man over another—until she is taken to wife by a man. Then she automatically favors her husband."

Hewitt glanced from one woman to the other. He was both fascinated and shocked. He was well aware of the long history of man and his dealings with women. But it was one thing to know of a condition that had existed in the past and quite another to see that these women actually regarded themselves as pawns. They didn't even realize how much degradation was implied by the words they were speaking.

Because of his knowledge of the past, it seemed to him that he understood this situation as no one aboard could possibly understand it.

Understanding it, he said firmly, "I'm sorry, ladies, for once you will have to make a choice among men. I can tell you right now, when I become captain, which of you I shall retain as my wife will depend entirely on how you show your choice at the moment when I ask you to do something on my behalf."

His words had a shock effect. A strange expression came into the face of Ruth. Ilsa suddenly looked shy. Ann Lesbee became very pale. Marianne stared at him with bright eyes.

Hewitt had the impression that all four were suddenly feeling timid, and there was a quality in them that he identified as old-fashionedness: a combination of extreme femininity, acceptance of male dominance, and a peculiar practicality.

Exactly how such a condition had come about—what dynamics were involved—could well be someone's project for a later social study.

At the moment, Hewitt said, "When Captain Gourdy returns, tell him that I was here and that I'm going now to the dormitory where the men are. I'll remain there and wait for him."

When Gourdy had this information conveyed to him half an hour later, he went to the detector room and switched on the scanners. He turned in on bedlam. The dormitory was filled with excited men who clearly believed that they would shortly be arriving at Earth. What shocked Gourdy was that his own men, whom he had placed as guards, were as aroused as anyone. They mingled with the prisoners, having apparently made up their minds that there were no further problems.

As he watched the wild scene, he realized belatedly that he had not taken into sufficient account the impact of Hewitt's appearance on the people of the ship. All that would now have to be rectified. Tensely, he considered what he might do. Then he called Harcourt in and showed him the scene.

He ordered, "You get down there as fast as you can. Take the elevator. Wait till no one is looking and slip into the

room. Then talk to each of our own men privately. Tell him
this is a very dangerous situation for us all. We have to remain in control till we get to Earth. If we lose command of
the situation, those prisoners may take their anger out on us.
Have our men leave the dormitory one at a time and come
up to the small assembly room. I'll talk to them there. Tell
'em no hard feelings. Everything is O.K."

He felt better when Harcourt hurried out of the room on
that mission.

He next tuned in on Lesbee. For several moments, he
watched that intent young man at his labors. He had a regret-
ful feeling. There were many things about Lesbee that he
liked, but he had a growing intuition that the former captain
was a permanent opponent, and that like Hewitt he would
have to be disposed of. Of course, that was for a later time.
Right now—

He called Lesbee on a communicator.

"Mr. Lesbee, I'm assigning you officer cabin Number
Three and I want you to go up to it right now because I'm
sending your wife over there. Who among the officers do you
think should be released in this situation?"

He took it for granted that Lesbee would know what situation.

Lesbee, who had his own plans, said promptly, "I wouldn't
let any of Browne's officers go, sir." Under his breath
he added: "Not while I'm doing all this meaningless work on
the engines." Aloud, he continued: "And since for obvious
reasons, you wouldn't want too many of mine loose during
this period of confusion, why not let me have Mr. Tellier to
help with these engines?" He thought: "That's really going
straight to the heart of the matter." He finished his answer to
Gourdy by saying respectfully, "Just to make sure that I'm
not misunderstanding, what precisely is the special situation?"

Gourdy explained about the excitement in the dormitory.
Then he said frankly, "Obviously, we can't let that develop
into a take-over by Hewitt. What do you think?"

Lesbee said, "I agree. Do you mind if I offer some advice?"

"Go ahead."

"What Hewitt has done is arouse hope. So we'll have to go
take a look at Earth. These wild people won't believe anything but their own eyes. Now, since it is to your interest to
continue to pursue the original purpose of the voyage,"—that

was nicely worded, it seemed to Lesbee—"I suggest the following: appear to accept Hewitt without argument. Agree to go to Earth. That will take the pressure off you right now. Later, we can discuss what to do next."

The apparent frankness of the discussion greatly relieved Gourdy. Once more he regretted that there seemed to be no way that justified his leaving Lesbee alive. But it was out of the question. The situation aboard the ship had become too complex. Mercy was not practicable.

Because he was a man in a hurry, Gourdy said quickly, "I'll have Mr. Tellier assigned an upper-level cabin and I shall return his wife to him also. And I'll do what you suggest as soon as I can brief my own men."

He broke the connection and stood up briskly. His confidence was back as he went out to where the women were finishing breakfast. He at once informed Ann Lesbee that she would return to her husband.

To his surprise, she burst into tears and showed visible unwillingness to leave. The other three women also wept. Ruth and Ilsa accompanied Ann into the second bedroom to help her get her things.

Marianne berated her husband. "It's not fair!" she sobbed, but there was anger in her voice. "We women have so little. You shouldn't send her away."

Since Gourdy was merely making a move as in a game, he considered the reactions he had observed with puzzled interest. "Look," he said, "I'm returning her to her handsome husband. What more can a woman want?"

"You're just talking silly!" said Marianne tearfully.

Gourdy couldn't wait to find out what was silly. But as he hurried out to deal with the severe emergency of Hewitt's arrival, it seemed to him that the last thing he had time for was the problem presented by a group of crying women.

32

"Now why," thought Lesbee, "does Gourdy want me to go up to my cabin right away, merely because my wife is being sent there?"

He decided not to go. It would be too easy to imprison him up there without anyone knowing.

As he reasoned it then, Lesbee pictured Captain Gourdy as trying to neutralize him till the situation in the dormitory was brought under control. When that was done, Gourdy would have to decide whom he would kill. He would need somebody to help him run the ship. As Lesbee saw it, it would be safer for Gourdy to use Miller and other Browne followers than himself. Because, apart from Miller's greater competence and training, the former first officer had it in his favor that he had never aspired to the captaincy. That, it seemed to Lesbee, would now be decisive in the mind of Gourdy. So it was he and his supporters who were doomed.

If the murders were done quietly following the excitement below, and if the arrangements with Miller were clear cut, then in a single decisive act the brilliant little former garden worker would have reduced his opponents once more to one: the stranger, Averill Hewitt.

. . . With so much attention focused on the intruder, probably Hewitt was temporarily safe. . . . It seemed to Lesbee that a clue to the intensity of Gourdy's desperation would be the speed with which he released Tellier—

Even as he had the thought, Tellier walked into the engine room.

Silently, the two friends shook hands. Lesbee made sure the spy signal was not flashing, then he asked in a deliberate tone: "Ready?"

Tellier's face took on a shocked expression. He said, "You mean—right now!"

"Now."

"But we're a hundredth of a light-year away—you said.

And we must still be traveling at practically the speed of light."

"It'll certainly take longer to slow down in the lifeboat than in the ship," said Lesbee. "But we've got to do it."

"Oh!" Then: "What about our wives?"

Lesbee was startled. He had not anticipated such near twelfth-hour objections. Impatient, tense, he caught Tellier's arm, pulled him. "We can't wait!"

Tellier held back. "I hate to leave Lou."

"She'll lose you one way or the other. If you stay, you'll be killed—"

"She won't understand."

So much concern over a woman was alien to Lesbee. "Since when has a woman ever understood anything!" he said irritably.

There must have been some sensibleness in that for Tellier, for he abandoned that line of resistance. Yet he still hesitated. He looked very downcast. "I guess I just can't bring myself to leave the ship," he confessed. "Why don't you stay and fight Gourdy scientifically?"

"Because the mass of the people aboard are for Gourdy."

"You could kill him outright. After all, he took the ship from you."

"Then I'd have to fight it out with his henchmen. Besides, if I killed him, then *I* might be subject to trial on Earth. I don't want to risk that. I've had my fill of being out in space."

"But there must be something we can do against an ignoramus like Gourdy, with all the power equipment on this ship!"

"Look!" said Lesbee, "you can't do anything, not anything, without support. My rebellion against Browne had almost everybody's sanction. Gourdy's rebellion against me was a surprise. But people were relieved and accepted it when Gourdy announced Earth was our destination. They still haven't realized that he can't go there, and we have no quick way of convincing them. Until they understand that, they'll never back another rebellion—"

"You make it all sound as if what that mob down there thinks or feels actually has some influence."

"When they know what they want, it makes all the difference."

"Then how come they stood for all this nonsense all these years?"

"Because they didn't think of it as nonsense—that's why."

"Then they're not very bright." ·

"True. But now they want to go to Earth and nothing can stop them. I don't want to be in the middle when the man who can't go—Gourdy—tries to hold them back. Smart as he is, he's so suspicious he won't think of it as a mass movement. And so, if he hasn't already killed us for other reasons—he'll kill us then because he'll think we're inciting the crowd against him. So let's go, man!"

The expression on Tellier's face had been softening for some seconds. Suddenly, the admiration was back. He grabbed Lesbee's arm in a spontaneous gesture of affection. "You really have thought everything out," he said. "John, you're a marvel."

He hesitated no longer but began to walk toward the door. "After all," he said, "if you're right, they'll be landing on Earth and I'll see Lou then."

Out in the corridor, Lesbee caught Tellier's sleeve, urging him forward. The two men broke into a run. They ran all the way to the airlock and climbed into the landing craft that Lesbee had surreptitiously readied. The machine, like the others, was fitted into a compartment in one of the walls. They settled breathlessly into the twin control chairs, and Lesbee pressed the switch that triggered the launch sequence.

The outer door of the big ship began to unscrew. Simultaneously, the inner door opened. The small craft slid out of its cradle and was propelled forward into the airlock. The inner door closed behind it. The air pumps started and swiftly sucked the air out of the lock.

As the outer door swung open a minute later, a powerful spring mechanism catapulted the small craft with the two men in it into space. When they had drifted several miles, Lesbee started the forward drives. Instantly, they began to decelerate. Off to one side, the *Hope of Man*—visible only by the dark shadow it made against the stars—seemed to forge ahead.

Lesbee knew that automatic warning lights were flickering on the big ship's two control boards. But he knew also that no person—at least, no person who understood—would be looking at the flashing signals.

Beside him, Tellier broke the silence. "Look at those stars," he said in a hushed tone. "We must be spinning."

Lesbee's gaze flashed to the stabilizer needles. They were steady. Frowning, he stared into the viewplate. And there was no doubt that something was wrong. The "fixed" stars seemed to be moving.

Gently, he took hold of the controls, gingerly moved them—first one way, then the other. The small ship responded perfectly, tilted to the left, then to the right. He brought the control back to dead center. The lifeboat came smoothly back into its electronically stabilized position.

Outside, the stars continued their slow movement. In all his years in space, Lesbee had never seen anything like it. In fact, one of the psychologically numbing realities of being out in space was that, almost literally, nothing ever changed position. As the years went by, a few "near" stars gradually shifted a few degrees. Only when the ship rotated did the stars seem to move at all.

Now, the entire stellar universe was visibly in motion. At least, that was his first impression. As he watched the fantastic scene, Lesbee slowly grew aware that the great nebulae, the distant star clouds, were as steady as ever.

That proved the movement of the stars was real. Even if the distant nebulae were in motion, that equaled the speed of the nearer stars, it wouldn't show. They were simply too far away. Even if they should start to move at scores of light-years a second, it would not be immediately detectable.

And since an instrument defect would show all the stars moving, not merely those that were close, the fact that those remote galaxies appeared to be stable *proved* that the star motion was not such a defect but a genuine event in space time.

"But," Lesbee wondered uneasily, "how can such a movement be explained?"

The only possibility—or so it seemed—was that the stars were actually speeding up in relation to the lifeboat—

He dared not utter that terrifying possibility to Tellier.

An hour went by. Two. Many.

In the darkness ahead was a star, which Lesbee believed was Earth's sun. What disturbed him was that the star began to dim. Although they were presumably approaching it, it grew smaller. And what confused Lesbee for a while was that even as it shrank it kept moving slowly across the face of

their viewing lens. Each time he would bring it back into focus—and the creeping action would occur again.

Lesbee was baffled. According to the figures on the veloc-
itor needles, they were going toward the solar system at a
speed that was still almost light-speed.

Yet the sun was visibly receding, as if it were speeding
away from them faster than they were approaching it.

If that were true, then the cross-movement meant that the
solar system was receding at an angle away from their craft.

Each passing minute, as Lesbee watched, the stars moved
faster in their already accelerated courses. Since they were
not all going in the same direction, they presented more and
more the appearance of chaos.

Minute by minute by minute, the scene grew wilder.

33

Gourdy had invited Hewitt to join him on the bridge.

With them were several of Browne's former officers, including Miller, Selwyn, and Mindel, and several scientists.
Two astronomers, Clyde Josephs who was chief of the astro-
nomical staff, and his chief assistant, Max Hook, were among
the latter.

In the background, five of Gourdy's henchmen stood. Each
of these five was armed with two blasters.

After they had gazed at the careening stars for at least a
minute, Hewitt grew aware that the chief astronomer's eyes
were beginning to shine.

"Gentlemen!" the man said in an awed tone. "We are witnessing a spectacle that surely no man ever dreamed he
would see—certainly no astronomer who has taken the rigidi-
ties of the space-time universe for granted."

He seemed to become aware of the tension in every person
who was watching him. His eyes widened. Then he looked at
Hewitt with an innocent, questioning expression, but it was
Gourdy he addressed.

"What is it you want to know, Captain?"

Gourdy made a strangled sound. "What's happening?" he asked explosively.

"The whole universe seems to be moving at millions of light-years a second." He stopped, as though he had just realized the fantastic thing that he had said, and stood blinking. He must have been in shock, for he went on, "I hope you will give me an opportunity to make a detailed study of the phenomenon."

He appeared to realize, from the choleric expression on Gourdy's face, that his request was not the exciting thing for Gourdy that it was for him.

He glanced around the circle of tense, staring eyes, and his somewhat round face took on an understanding expression.

"Don't be alarmed, gentlemen! If you have some fear that the stars are going to run away from us, or that time will run out for us—don't worry. This can probably go on for billions of years."

Again, he paused. Again, he must have realized that he was still not making a warm place for himself in the hearts of the dozen men who were watching him so grimly.

It was Hewitt who suddenly relaxed and said in a friendly tone, "Mr. Josephs, the figure you have used—millions of light-years—indicates that we are in trouble as no human beings have ever been. At this moment I'm frightened. Are we ever going to see our own people again, and if so, how are we going to do it? This is what concerns us."

Josephs stood stock-still, blinking. Then he said, "Oh!" And in a subdued tone. "The sun is only moving away from us slowly. I would venture to say that that proves that what we are witnessing is not entirely a speed phenomenon."

Hewitt said, startled, "But that would mean a time expansion of absolutely incredible proportions. I can't even imagine it."

Josephs said apologetically, "Perhaps the sooner I begin my study—"

"But where are the planets?" Gourdy yelled. "That's what we want to know. What's happened to Earth, Mars, Venus, Jupiter and—and—the others? They aren't there."

He was more perturbed about that than about the speed. Earth *was* his ultimate goal. His special situation required that he go there more slowly than the others desired.

But he wanted Earth to be there when he finally arrived.

Once more Josephs was apologetic. "They probably are

there, sir, but orbiting around the sun at such a high velocity we can't see them. I imagine that if we could look closely enough we'd see rings of light. The superspeed cameras aboard will undoubtedly be able to obtain some kind of picture."

Gourdy said from between clenched teeth, "Take 'em. Take the pictures, damn it, and send them to me."

The photographs—which were delivered to Gourdy's desk later that day—showed all the planets. Josephs had appended a note:

> Dear Captain:
> The solar system is speeding away from us at an angle. This angle derives from the fact that it is still heading toward Aries, and we are approaching from another direction.
> In this connection, we are entitled to consider Mr. Hewitt's story of how the *Hope of Man* entered the solar system, caught up to Earth, and entered the atmosphere in such a fashion that we seemed to move at only a few miles an hour. Yet, so far as the ship was concerned, we were traveling faster than light.
> Now that we have slowed down, apparently the solar system is pulling away from us. This is logical in the frame of that "earlier" relationship.
> Apparently, as we decelerated below light-speed, our time orientation altered drastically, but spatially we seem to be still operating in the same general area.
> However, if we are not to lose sight of the sun, I suggest we speed up somewhat—and then decide what to do next.
>   (signed) CLYDE JOSEPHS

Gourdy riffled through the photographs with impatient fingers. He was about to put them down when an oddity about one of the pictures struck him. He drew it out of the pack and stared at it with a frown.

The camera had taken a picture angling across a part of the curved outer hull of the *Hope of Man*. In the distance, this starry scene was of a portion of the sky. It was bright and beautiful with points of lights—thousands of distant suns. On the back of the picture, Josephs had written in connection with this part of the scene: "Looking toward Aries, toward which the solar system is moving."

That part was understandable, obvious.

But there was a whitish blotch across the lower part of the photograph. At that point, the curving surface of the ship was already falling away. The blotch seemed to be an extension of a condition that came up from the ship, below the range of the camera.

About this phenomenon, Josephs had noted on the back, "I have no idea what the semicircular shape is. It looks like too much light got onto the film. In view of our unusual matter-state, I decided not to make the automatic assumption that it was merely a defect."

Gourdy couldn't make anything out of it either. So he shrugged presently and put it aside. He felt incompetent in the face of so many unusual conditions to make any kind of a scientific judgment. But he was as convinced as ever that he was the logical person to supervise the research that would have to be done. As he saw it, the scientists would have to report to him. He would decide what to do, and when.

He said to Harcourt, who had brought the photos, "We got plenty of scientific brains to take care of our scientific problems."

Thus, lightly, he dismissed a situation that had no parallel in human experience.

He saw now, clearly, that this condition was the opportunity he had been seeking.

"Call everybody up to the main assembly room," he commanded. "See that the boys are armed, and tell 'em to act and look as if they can take care of anything and anybody."

"You want everybody?" Harcourt asked, incredulous. "All those guys from downstairs, too!"

"Everybody. Meeting right after dinner."

At the meeting, Gourdy had the projectionist show the photos, and he had Clyde Josephs explain what they meant.

When that was done, Gourdy stepped forward. "Now, folks," he said, "what this really means is that we won't be landing till we solve the problem. I promise this. The best scientific and engineering brains aboard will be assigned to the task and"—he indicated Hewitt, who sat in the front row below him—"I'm sure Mr. Hewitt will contribute what he can from his over-all knowledge of the ship."

He beckoned Hewitt. "Will you come up here, sir?" he asked graciously.

Hewitt climbed onto the stage grimly. He was disturbed by

the skill with which Gourdy was manipulating the meeting in his own favor. He glanced questioningly at Gourdy.

Gourdy said courteously, "Mr. Hewitt, will you tell all of these people how and under what conditions you came aboard?"

When Hewitt had done so, Gourdy said, "In your opinion, is there any chance of using your method in reverse to get these people to Earth?"

Even if there was, it was the last thing that Hewitt—with *his* purposes—would have admitted.

Aloud he said, "Since we don't even know exactly what happened, the answer has to be that it's impossible. I've tried to imagine the time-space condition that existed when I came aboard the *Hope of Man*—what, for example, was the relationship in terms of physics and chemistry between me and the ship? I cannot get a satisfactory concept. My suggestion is the same as Mr. Josephs'—that we catch up with the solar system, and then take our next move on the basis of what we observe at that time."

Gourdy stepped forward beside Hewitt. He was smiling, but alarm bells were ringing inside him. Although he could see no harm in the actual suggestion, he suddenly suspected a conspiracy. The fact that Josephs and Hewitt had made the same recommendation seemed significant and sinister. He had a feeling that the scientists understood something that he didn't.

At the moment, he saw that he had no alternative but to accept it. He said loudly, "I hereby authorize Mr. Hewitt and Mr. Miller to accelerate this ship to match velocities with the solar system."

He turned to Hewitt, and with apparent openness said, "What about the repair Mr. Lesbee was doing on the engine?"

Hewitt had already examined the engines and recognized the repair for what it was. He said smoothly, "Only the instrument panels have been removed so far, and we should be able to replace them by the time the sleep period begins."

"Then act!" said Gourdy in the decisive tone that he considered necessary to reassure the people of the ship at this special meeting.

Thus the assembly came to its end.

Back in his cabin, Gourdy settled into his chair with savage satisfaction and gazed up at Harcourt. "And now," he said, "we've got to get rid of Hewitt. What he did there did him no good, but it was a try."

The quick, earlier suspicion had become a solid certainty in his mind.

He added, "Hewitt is our only danger now, since Lesbee took off."

Thought of Lesbee made him shake his head in wonderment. "That guy Lesbee really had a head on his shoulders. He had me figured, all right. But I'm kinda glad he got away—if he did; maybe he's lost out there in that spinning universe." He broke off: "Here, have a sip of this!"

Ilsa had been pouring wine while he talked. He ignored her as one might a servant. He was unaware that his attitude toward the women was changing. More and more, he treated them as if they were total nonentities.

Paying no attention to Ilsa, he said, "Killing Hewitt should be made to look like an accident. But don't waste any time. Do it just before morning. Best thing I can think of is, make it look as if his machine short-circuited in some way and exploded."

"That'll be pretty hard for me to put over." Harcourt spoke doubtfully.

Gourdy was contemptuous. "Don't be a nut. It doesn't matter how something is done, just so's you leave yourself a loophole. Something that confuses these poor dopes is all you need. And then you make it damned dangerous for anyone to be suspicious."

There was what seemed to be a continuing resisting expression on Harcourt's face. Gourdy scowled at his henchman.

"Look—" he said flatly, "we've got to do it. Don't give me any argument!"

Harcourt protested, "I'm not arguing, boss. I'm just thinking how to do it. Since you didn't take any of that stuff away from him, who knows what he's got in that space capsule. My idea is I'll just blow it up, but I'll have to see how to do it."

Gourdy said, "I let him keep it because I didn't want him to have any suspicion that I was going to move against him. So now we use it against him."

"The way I've got it," said Harcourt, more confident now, "I'll brief some of the guys. Then I'll go down to the engine room when Miller and Hewitt start the acceleration. And I'll stick with Hewitt from that time on. I'll follow him to his room. I'll wait in the hallway outside until the other guys join me. My idea is, we'll go in some time during the last half of the sleep period and catch him in bed. O.K?"

"Sounds perfect," said Gourdy.

It was at that point that the woman slipped out of the room. Although she went quietly, her departure brought her to Gourdy's awareness.

He said, "As soon as Hewitt is out of the way, I'm taking over these women. I've already had Lesbee's wife brought back. Since she didn't want to go in the first place, I decided to return her to the status of captain's wife. If that makes her happy, I can't complain."

He gazed up at the big man cynically. "Now listen, I'm giving each of you fellows permission to take on a second woman. I warn you, though. Don't just grab one. Tell the men to look over a few and then come to me. We'll decide between us which one. We can't monkey with the wives of men we need, and there'd be trouble if somebody took one of the young girls. But we'll figure it out and keep it damn secret for a while."

Harcourt's eyes were glistening. "That fellow, Tellier—his wife! Can I have her?"

"She's yours—after tomorrow," said Gourdy, casually. "Now, get!"

Harcourt got.

34

Surprisingly, Hewitt found a brief comradeship with Miller. The two men submerged any personal animosity they might otherwise have felt, in their mutual discovery of how to operate the matched-drive system.

They examined the almost magical alteration that Dzing had made in the giant Bev system for accelerating the particles so that they actually expanded.

They were astounded by the simplicity of the method of particle removal by the process of tilting the antigravity plates.

By this means, the original method of maintaining a one-g antigravity could be amplified, theoretically, to any limit—hundreds, even thousands, of g's.

The discovery, though highly stimulating, was also sobering; for there was now so much power that it had to be dealt with cautiously.

They carefully repeated Lesbee's earlier tests, bringing the acceleration gradually up to twelve g's while they balanced the antigravity at eleven g's. The perfection of it made their eyes glisten, and when the programming was complete, with acceleration set to continue at the one-g differential, they shook hands in the most friendly fashion.

Miller at this point announced that he had to report to Gourdy, and departed. Because of Harcourt, Hewitt did not leave the security of the engine room at once. Something about the big brute—he had a morbid intuition.

As his first act of defense, he slipped a small wrench into one pocket. Then, while pretending to examine what was inside one of the panels that Lesbee had removed, he loosened from its socket and put into his other pocket a special tube. . . . The gas in the tube was a rare, potent poison. If threatened, he could throw it on the floor at Harcourt's feet. At very least, the man would get a whiff. Hewitt would then have time to attack him with the wrench.

It was the best he could do under the circumstances.

As he headed back to the officer's cabin, which he had ostentatiously been assigned by Gourdy. Hewitt was aware of Harcourt following him. . . . It was very disturbing in those silent, empty corridors.

So he stopped, finally, and waited for the man to catch up with him. When Harcourt's lumbering gait brought him close, Hewitt said, "Why don't we walk together?"

The man mumbled something. But he offered no objection as Hewitt fell in step beside him. When they came to Hewitt's cabin, Hewitt unlocked the door, aware that the large man had paused also and was waiting.

He turned, and asked frankly, "Is there anything I can do for you?"

Harcourt pretended open honesty. "I'm supposed to keep an eye on you, Mr. Hewitt, and see that you don't get into or cause trouble. I'll be in the room across this hall with my door open. O.K.?"

It sounded. O.K. But Hewitt entered his apartment with an unhappy feeling. The fact was he could not delay.

His mind seethed with schemes. But what he swiftly settled on was that he would simply get into his tank suit and drive down the corridor. If Harcourt fired a blaster at him, then he would run the man down.

The suit itself was built to withstand bullets or blasts from handarms.

The decision made, he started toward the space bedroom, where he had the machine—and stopped!

A soft sound . . . ! From his own bedroom!

Hewitt snatched for the wrench—then let his hand slide away as the woman, Ruth, appeared in the bedroom doorway. She put a finger to her lips, a cautioning gesture.

Quickly, she whispered to him that Ilsa had overheard: the plot to murder him. She ended her account. "We had to choose. I chose you!"

Hewitt, whose mind had started to reach past what she had said, came reluctantly back to the woman, her words, her—choice!

He was embarrassed. With him, what had brought her here had been a move as in a game. Simply and forthrightly, he believed in monogamy. Her flushed cheeks and the shy way she avoided looking into his eyes told him that it was no game to her and the others.

The woman spoke again. "I knew I would have to come here before Harcourt and you returned. So now you'll have to think of something to do with me . . . I brought this to help!"

She reached into a fold in her dress, produced a small blaster, and held it out to him. Hewitt took the weapon gratefully. The feel of it in his hand eased the awful chill of the murder plan she had described.

It also changed his own plan.

Quickly, he explained to her what he wanted her to do: hide in his bedroom, wait till Harcourt and he entered the adjoining bedroom, then slip out. "Be sure," Hewitt finished, "to take off your shoes, so you can go silently—"

She started obediently for the bedroom door; then she stopped. Hesitantly, she faced him, said simply, "Am I chosen?"

A lump came into Hewitt's throat. Gazing at her, he thought: "Space did this to these women. The awful emptiness of space reduced them, gave them a sense of loss that made even the best of them vulnerable to total control."

He divined that words were not enough in this situation. This woman needed to be touched. He stepped up to her, took one of her hands in his, and placed his other hand on her shoulder, squeezing it slightly. "You are completely chosen!" he said softly.

The expression of relief that came into her fine-featured face was something to see. Abruptly, she was an accepted woman, calm, practical. "I'd better go!" she said. She stared at him earnestly. "You'll be all right?"

Hewitt released her hand. "I'll do my best," he said. "I'll see you later."

She whispered, "We're all waiting for you!" She turned and went into the bedroom, pushing the door almost shut—

Hewitt slipped the blaster in with the wrench, walked over, and opened the corridor door. He called across the hallway to where he could see Harcourt sitting in a chair just inside the open door of the apartment there, "Will you come in here and give me a hand, Mr. Harcourt?"

The big man climbed to his feet and slouched to the door, stared insolently at Hewitt. "What do you want?"

"I need a hand here with my machine."

"Going some place?" Harcourt asked.

But he came over, looking puzzled and undecided. He was not a man who could easily change from one plan to another. At Hewitt's request, he walked into the spare bedroom.

"Hey!" he said, as he saw the blaster that Hewitt was pointing at him. His whole body stiffened. There was shock and horror in his face.

Slowly, he put up his hands.

Minutes later, Hewitt was guiding his tank suit along the corridor at its top speed. He was a man in a hurry.

35

In his excitement, Lesbee shook Tellier awake.

"Hey! I've figured out the true nature of the universe."

The thin, intellectual face of his friend seemed to gain a little color. The pale, watery skin looked more alive. "You've what?"

As Tellier sat up sleepily, Lesbee repeated his statement, adding: "With what I've analyzed, we can do anything: land on Earth, retake the ship . . . anything."

Tellier turned red. "For God's sake, John," he whispered, "are you serious? You know what respect I have for your ideas when you tell me you mean them."

"Listen——" said Lesbee. "First, the facts as we've seen them, or had them accurately described——"

He thereupon outlined the aspects of the long voyage related to the physics of space: the initial impossibility of accelerating particles to light velocity, the discovery through the Karn of the correct pattern——

He continued his summation: "Hewitt's story of the *Hope of Man* arriving in the solar system in a special matter-state, which turned out to mean that the ship was traveling faster than light in some space of its own. Finally, as the ship reduced to light-speed, Hewitt was precipitated into the world of the ship——

"These are the facts, aren't they?" Lesbee demanded.

Tellier nodded, wide-eyed.

"Actually, there are more points," Lesbee continued. "For example, the time and pressure ratios were 973 to one. But the outside of the ship remained round. And the corridors inside were only three to one. I understand all that now."

"But what's the practical vaule?"

"Watch!" said Lesbee.

He disappeared.

. . . Vanished inside a small craft millions of miles from anywhere. . . . Tellier was frantically looking around, when

144

he heard a sound behind him. He whirled. Lesbee stood there, a triumphant grin on his face.

The smile faded and was succeeded by a grim expression. "We're going back to the ship!" Lesbee said.

"Whatever for?" Tellier was astonished.

The steely eyes gazed at him. "For your wife—for mine— To make sure that the ship lands. . . . We had to forget all that when it was life or death. But that doesn't apply any more."

Tellier grasped his hand gratefully. "Good man!" he said. Then he stepped back. "For God's sake, tell me what it is you've discovered."

"First, let's get started," said Lesbee. He turned to the control board, went on, "Now, theoretically, it should be possible to go there, literally, in a moment. The machine could. But remember what happened to Hewitt—the squeeze feeling. Human cells would not long survive instantaneity. So we've got to accept that life has to have a little time."

"But—"

"The universe is a lie," said Lesbee, a few moments later. *"That's the secret!* Listen—"

It was a subjective plenum that he described then, consisting essentially of levels of motion. In that universe, life had got its start by holding onto bits and pieces of dead matter. From this precarious vantage point, like a bug clinging to a straw in a whirlpool, it surveyed the heavens and itself.

Tentatively, it explored the great flows of motion all around, enclosed itself in sealed containers so that it could confront the energy at the lower levels, at the higher levels, and beyond the light-speed.

Here, in an environment of infinite expansion and zero size, was the real norm of time and space. "Below," was the nether darkness of stopped motion and matter. "Above" was the infinite, timeless light of foreverness.

As life in the sealed containers—spaceships—crossed the dividing line and entered the norm, the barriers went down. It was as if a man had crawled out of a black well, and now he stood on the meadow, and gazed into the bright blue of the sky. The laws governing the meadows were different from, though related to, those in the well.

Lesbee said, "We could theoretically go instantly from no motion to millions of times the speed of light. But as I've said, from a practical point of view, the inner motions of cells hold us back a little. We fear at some level that the movement is threatening, and we grab for a handrail, and hold on for dear life."

He finished, "My thought is, naturally, that we respect that feeling of the cells, and proceed with caution, but proceed."

Tellier stared at him blankly. "I don't get it," he said. "All right, so the matter-state beyond light is the norm. I've been there, too. Nothing that I could notice happened to me."

"That is because you lay very still during the whole time," said Lesbee. "That's because you weren't tuned in to a landing device that could operate on thought impulses."

Tellier looked at him blankly. Then he blurted out: "You don't mean to tell me you left that connected all this time?"

"No. But that's the one thing I reconnected when I was fooling around with the drive controls."

As he explained it, he had been striving to think of every possible precaution before they left the ship. And so he had come early to the thought that the arrangement whereby the lifeboat-landing mechanism operated through the controls of the *Hope of Man*—exactly as he had used it with Dzing—would enable them to control the big vessel from a distance if necessary.

"It was really all just scheming," he confessed. "I pictured Miller being used to follow us or something—and so I did one thing that might give us control at a key moment. I had no other purpose in mind than that. All the rest of this came when I was reviewing, among other things, what happened to Dzing when I operated that switch."

"Didn't he just blow up?"

"That's what it looked like."

"The corridor was a shambles; the explosion literally almost dissolved him. The pieces found were like pieces of fluff, without weight."

"Don't you think that was odd?" Lesbee was smiling faintly but tautly.

"Well—" Tellier looked baffled.

Gazing at the other's face, Lesbee realized anew how difficult it was for people to have creative thoughts. His own brain had evidently attained some peak of quick comprehension from his years of operating under the basically hostile control of the Brownes. Overstimulated by fear, rage, envy, feelings of the rightness of his cause . . . he had seen the whole picture, as he now understood it, in a single flash of vivid comprehension.

Tellier, lacking that background, would have to have the explanation spelled out for him.

Lesbee hesitated before the fact of the other's inability. For the first time he questioned his impulse to share with Tellier.

He had been sitting on the edge of the control chair. The doubt brought him to his feet. He stood, eyes narrowed, considering what it was he had to say.

What remained to tell was fantastic but simple, unquestionably related to the basic structure of the universe—but explainable. When he had activated Dzing's self-destruct system, he had destroyed the robot. The evidence was the shattered wall and the indented ceiling and floor of the corridor where it had happened. But the Karn had been at the norm period when it happened.

Throughout, Dzing had operated and functioned outside the space-time limitations of the *Hope of Man*. The robot had been unaffected by four g's of acceleration. That could not be explained by energy flows. Even more important, the light weight of what was left of the robot body fitted what Browne had said about the nature of matter at light-speed. The Lorentz-Fitzgerald Contraction Theory applied in all its remarkable meaning.

And so he had—while Tellier slept—reached into his pocket and pressed a control button of the landing mechanism; and he had let its energy amplify his thought.

Instantly, he was in the norm state of the universe, at light-speed and beyond. He had set the time ratio at 973 to one, because of Hewitt's experience. Lesbee decided that the cells of a human body—perhaps of all bodies—had some natural balance at that ratio. He preferred not to go counter to such a native state of being without a lot of experimentation.

That first time, he had stared down at Tellier, eager to wake him up, and tell him the great discovery. Now, the excitement faded, he changed his mind.

He turned, and faced his friend, and said quietly, "Armand, I can see I've given you as much new data as your brain should absorb at one time."

Tellier did not reply. The high excitement of what he had seen and heard was fading from him. There was something in his friend's manner, a certain hardness, the presence of which had always surprised him. It surprised him again now. Suddenly, he saw that such a momentous discovery by a man who, despite his many likable qualities, was at heart a dictator ... was not a good thing.

Lesbee was speaking once more, his voice friendly, his manner kind, as always. He said, "I'll tell you the rest at some later time."

But he never did.

36

A bright light gleamed in Gourdy's eyes. He stirred in his sleep then awakened with a start.

His bedroom was brightly lighted. He blinked the brightness away and saw Hewitt and half a dozen men dressed in the uniforms of—Gourdy stared unbelieving. He recognized the gray-blue cloth from old films:

... Space Parol ... !

One of the uniformed men, a stern-faced older person, said in a deep baritone, "Mr. Gourdy, you are under arrest and will be taken off this ship."

Two of the uniformed men stepped forward and grabbed him, brought his wrists together. There was a gleam of metal, the cold feel of it on his skin. Handcuffs clicked with a steely sound.

Gourdy managed to sit up at this point. He was still struggling to shake off sleep. As he stared down at the gleaming metal things, he had the feeling that he was having a nightmare.

To one side, a uniformed man said to Marianne: "You may accompany your husband to Earth, if you wish, Mrs. Gourdy."

"No, no, no—" Her voice was high-pitched, unnatural. "I'll stay right here—"

"That is your privilege, madame. It is Mr. Hewitt's decision that the voyage shall go on. You are one of the few aboard who may choose to stay or go."

Strong hands were now pulling Gourdy to his feet. "Come along!" somebody commanded.

He made his fisrt real resistance. "Hey!" he said. He tried to jerk away.

The stern-faced man made a gesture to the two men who were holding him. Without a word, they picked him up and carried him out of the bedroom into the main room.

As Gourdy's glance flicked over the room, he saw that the three other women—Ruth, Ilsa, and Ann—were in their dressing gowns, huddled in the doorway of the second bedroom.

Even as he watched, a woman in the uniform of a Space Patrol officer went over to them, and said, "Please get dressed, ladies!"

Ruth nodded and drew the other two gently back into the room, out of sight. The door closed.

Gourdy saw now that two uniformed men stood at the corridor door. They stepped aside. A few moments later, Harcourt, one other of his men, and four Space Patrolmen, entered. Gourdy's two henchmen were handcuffed to each other. They appeared bewildered and at first they did not seem to notice Gourdy.

The patrolmen held a low-voiced conversation with Hewitt, then they went out.

During the next hour, all eighteen of Gourdy's men were captured and brought to the captain's cabin. When they were all there in a sullen group, Hewitt motioned the patrol officers aside and addressed the prisoners.

"That photograph with the splotch of light on it was the key," he began. "It was not defective, a fact which I began to suspect right away. When I looked at the enlargement as it was projected onto a screen by Astronomer Josephs, it occurred to me that I was looking at a section of my own salvage ship, the *Molly D.*

"And when I opened the airlock and went through, there it was, big as life."

He continued: "The scientific reason for such a dual space-time condition is not yet known. But there are several unique features in this situation.

"For example, when I looked out from the bridge of the *Hope of Man* yesterday, the solar system was many, many quadrillions of miles away. Yet from a porthole of the *Molly D.*, I saw that in some time fashion, *it* is well inside the solar system. In fact, I could see Earth, and it seemed to be going along normally.

"We may surmise that some of the beings you saw out in space have solved these space-time confusions, and obviously the *Hope of Man* must remain in space until the problem is solved for the human race also. To help us solve this problem, several leading scientists have volunteered to come aboard. We shall also have a full complement of other scholars and experts and, of course, a Space-Patrol unit to keep order. Some of these men will bring their families. Others are single.

"As soon as they are aboard, the *Molly D* will cast off, and we shall be alone again. As for you men—"

He paused to make sure that he had their full attention, then continued:

"As far as I know, no one will be charged with unlawful acts. The history of the ship is regarded as a sociological and not a criminal phenomenon. But we don't want you on the ship."

Hewitt turned to the patrol chief, said quietly, "I think that about does it."

When Gourdy and his cronies had been herded out of the apartment, Hewitt confronted the women who were now fully dressed.

"Be calm," he said. "Everything will be all right. Why don't you have breakfast? I have many things to do."

He went out without explaining further. He anticipated that the women would have a problem adjusting. But, then, many others would have the same problem.

Law and order were about to come aboard the *Hope of Man*.

Hewitt remained away from the captain's cabin during the entire transformation period that followed. . . . On the eighth day, a patrol craft arrived with the first of the new passengers.

Among the arrivals was the redoubtable Peter Linden. "Young man," he said to Hewitt, with eyes that twinkled, though his face was serious, "the unsuspected existence of so many unusual space-time conditions finally made me take a look at the mathematics of John Lesbee I. I have accordingly advised the government of the Combined Western Powers that his theory and proof have shaken my confidence and that I believe that something will happen, that the sun may indeed take on—what is the famous phrase that was so often ridiculed?—'some of the aspects of a Cepheid Variable.' We'd better figure out something to do about that."

Hewitt, who had years of frustration behind him on this subject, was silent. He had no facile solution either.

37

Lesbee and Tellier arrived at the *Hope of Man* almost in no time. He had brought the entire craft up to 973-to-one time ratio, and so their coming was not visible to those aboard.

At the airlock, he reduced the ratio to ship time. His purpose was to enter quickly, which was done. But he was nervous now. As soon as the small craft was stowed away, he activated its airlock, emerged from it—and only he stepped up to the higher time ratio.

In this state he went directly to the bridge, and, with a small power tool that he had brought with him to fast time, released the relay that had snapped up when the lifeboat entered its compartment.

Next, he headed for Tellier's apartment and literally materialized before the eyes of Tellier's wife. It took a while then to give reassurances, to make clear what he wanted; the woman remained in a disturbed emotional condition longer than he had anticipated. She kept closing her gray eyes tight, then opening them and staring at him as if in disbelief. And she talked steadily about how she had missed her husband.

When she did grow calmer, it was only to break out on a new level of compulsive chatter. This time Lesbee learned about the coming of the strangers. He could have become interested at that point; could have questioned her closely. But even that, he decided, could wait.

At last, she subsided, smiled wanly, and said, "What do you want me to do?"

He wanted her to get her clothes together and accompany him to the landing craft.

That also took time, but presently he had her in the life-boat, and he left her there with her husband.

Lesbee returned to look over the ship. This time he saw the newcomers. He found vantage positions from which he could examine them; Lou Tellier had been singularly unclear as to who they were.

. . . Patrol officers and civilians.

He traced them to the *Molly D,* and examined the situation there with some interest, tried to analyze what was going on. Since a considerable amount of luggage had been moved into cabins, and several families were already aboard, he realized with amazement that the intention was to continue the voyage.

Lesbee hid in an empty case and accompanied one of the *Molly D's* landing craft back to Earth.

And so he stood on a planet, stood with his two feet on soil, on pavement. For most of the first day he wandered in a normal state around the streets, watched the traffic, read the papers. Reverting briefly to high-time rate, he went into a bank vault where a responsible officer was getting money. Lesbee helped himself to a thousand dollars and departed. It would be months before anyone would discover that it was gone.

He came one to one, timewise, checked in at a magnificent hotel, and ate the finest meal he had ever had. Afterwards, in the hotel bar, he picked up a good-looking young woman who was also staying at the hotel. Late in the evening, they retired to his apartment. For several hours he listened to her chatter, striving to orient himself to the world. In the morning they had breakfast together, he made her a suitable gift, and went his way; she hers.

The papers that morning reported that Gourdy had been rearrested.

Lesbee read the charge with alarm. The Space Board had decided that it would extend its hold across a century of time, down five generations—claiming that only thus could space travel be kept orderly. No matter how long the voyage, people must learn that if they did not in the end accept the "natural"—the word was actually used—development of authority aboard a space vessel, they would be punished to the full extent of the law.

What this reasoning told Lesbee was that his own rebellion

might be illegal. The Browne take-over could easily be considered natural.

Suddenly, he had two choices only: Remain on Earth, live quietly, call no attention to himself. . . . Go back to the ship, take it away from Hewitt, and resume the voyage. . . .

Since a man with his special information should not remain silent, the first choice had no meaning.

But what really decided him was that several newspapers carried Peter Linden's reasoning on the possible validity of John Lesbee I's theory of change in the sun. . . . It was carefully done by Linden. He predicted that there would be plenty of time to consider the matter and act on it.

Lesbee, who had read his ancestor's account in the ship's records, recalled that his great-great-grandfather had decided that the change would occur—as Lesbee remembered it—in from six to ten years.

He did a quick mental calculation, and realized anxiously: "Good lord, we're already into that period!"

He switched to superfast time rate and went to the prison for a talk with Gourdy. After the shock effect of his abrupt materialization in the cell had passed—they talked.

. . . Agreement: retake the ship! Lesbee to be captain, Gourdy his chief lieutenant. To Lesbee, it was a dangerous but necessary compromise. One man could not capture a vessel by himself, and hold it.

He took Gourdy and his followers into the high time speed with him. They boarded the *Molly D* landing craft, carried out of the little vessel the contents of several packing cases, then hid on a normal time basis inside those cases. So that when the craft took off that night it had aboard twenty unsuspected passengers.

Because of these activities, Lesbee did not see the evening papers that printed Hewitt's radioed protest on the arrest of Gourdy. Newspaper editorials supported Hewitt's position. . . . Shortly before midnight, the Space Board yielded to the mounting opposition and promised to reconsider the matter at the next meeting a week hence.

But it was too late.

Back in the *Hope of Man*, Lesbee installed Gourdy and his men in a storeroom that would not normally be opened, and the equipment in it used, until a landing was made on an alien planet. . . . It was agreed the group would remain quiet until all connection was severed between the interstellar vessel and the *Molly D*.

Technician Lesbee disconnected the wiring from the control room to the listening and scanning devices within the walls. He brought the men food and comforts: cots, blankets, games and books—there were a hundred thousand new books aboard.

When he was with Gourdy's group, and listened to their coarse humor, Lesbee felt uneasy. But each time, he fought off his doubts because there was no other solution.

Lesbee saw no difference between the decision of the Space Board to arrest and try Gourdy for murder, and the decision Gourdy had made to kill the two technicians and the scientist. By its action, the Space Board intended to pressure future space travelers into submitting to control of appointed kings. Gourdy's intent had been to frighten anyone who opposed his being king.

—No difference! Thus reasoned John Lesbee V. And his jaw tightened with the determination to carry through on his personal take-over plan.

While he waited for the *Molly D* to cast off, Lesbee watched what was happening on the ship—

Changes were occurring. Science had come aboard. Psychologists were lecturing. Sociologists traced the history of the ship for those who had been too close to the actuality to see its significance. The military aspect—which had been fastened onto the people virtually at the last minute when the voyage originally began—was replaced by a system worked out, not by military experts but by scientific people.

From a hidden point on a balcony overlooking the assembly room, Lesbee listened to a lecture by Hewitt on the difference between a scientific approach and other systems. Among other things, Hewitt said:

"Scientists are an amazing breed. On the one hand, they are conservative. But within the frame of their training, a group of scientists represent truth, integrity, order, sensitivity, and sensibility on the highest level. . . ."

He compared the extreme difficulty of obtaining top scientists at the beginning of the voyage, with the ease he had had in obtaining any number of volunteers on this occasion. The reason: a ship returned from a voyage of over a hundred years represented a clear and immediate problem. Every aspect of that problem had aroused scientific interest and enthusiasm—

Lesbee watched the result of that enthusiasm. Humanitarian laws were codified. There were a police force, judges, a jury system. A captain, yes—Hewitt—but he became the administrator of the law through the system. He had his rights and duties. . . .

Universal equal education was set up, with an administering board and teachers with personal rights and privileges. . . .

Lesbee listened to Hewitt explain in another lecture why only on a ship could such a complete, perfect system be established. Outside force and technology, scientifically altruistic, could move in upon such a limited world as the *Hope of Man* and in a short time create a model system.

Hewitt explained that among nations on Earth there was no comparable altruistic outside force. Victors in wars, motivated by hatred and the need to control, degrade, despoil, and punish—were virtually the only outside forces human beings had ever known. The defeated knew their fate, held still for the disaster through fear, built up their own hatred, waited their chance—which usually came through the conniving of international politics.

Lesbee's first impulse was to consider Hewitt naïve.

Hewitt didn't seem to be aware that, while the ship's inhabitants accepted their rights, there was already muttering against the duties.

And that the men were outraged by the attitude of the newcomers which implied that the women aboard had not been treated right.

Presently, Lesbee found himself wondering if Hewitt's apparent unawareness was not part of a skillful game, another way to power.

While all this was developing, the *Molly D* cast off.

For Lesbee, when he heard this, all the turmoil aboard the ship became as nothing.

The time had come for his take-over.

38

Lesbee had a strong impulse to go and see Tellier before he did anything.

But he recognized the desire as a weakness. He actually thought, "Maybe I want him to talk me out of this." He did not go.

For a few moments before he came down from high to even time, Lesbee stared at the twisted caricature figures of the Gourdy gang. It was an unhappy stare. He disliked this whole group. But unfortunately these were his only possible allies at this stage.

Most of these negative feelings were still strangely heavy on him a little later as he explained the situation to Gourdy. There were so many doubts—"It's almost," Lesbee thought, "as if I consider what I'm about to do an outdated solution. Perhaps I've let all that scientific propaganda affect me."

He reassured himself that Hewitt was simply another power seeker.

The faraway expression in Lesbee's eyes did not escape Gourdy.

It was the moment of carelessness he had been waiting for all these days. He glanced significantly at Harcourt, who, by instruction, had watched the two men alertly during their discussion.

Lesbee sighed. "Better start the attack on the ship," he thought, "and get it over with." His intention was to begin by disarming everybody aboard.

At that final instant he caught Harcourt's movement, and his fingers closed convulsively over the control device, squeezed it in a grip of iron.

It was the last thing he ever did.

The blow of energy from Harcourt's blaster caught him in the side of the head and upper shoulder.

Blackout! . . . death! . . . instantly.

156

Pressing the control button knocked him into another time ratio barely short of the ratio related to light-speed, about the same as Hewitt's original 973 to one.

There he lay as dead as any man would ever be.

Gourdy gazed down at the twisted body. In his sharp way, he had observed the one thing Lesbee did consistently in connection with his fantastic disappearing act: the putting of his hand in his pocket. There was no other repeated action.

So—Gourdy had reasoned—Lesbee had some device there by which he was able to become invisible.

He said, "Roll him over and see what he's got in that pocket."

The dead body was lifted as if it were made of feathers.

A moment later, Harcourt triumphantly handed Gourdy the control device.

Gourdy pressed the button and turned the switch, one after the other, to the three positions. Nothing happened. Maybe this wasn't it. . . . They searched Lesbee's pockets frantically for some other mechanism, but found nothing.

Again and again, Gourdy manipulated the three-stage switch. Since it was a thought-amplifying device that reacted to certain thoughts only, there was no response.

Baffled, finally, he stared at the almost weightless, fragile body of his dead enemy; and in him were those bitter, hopeless feelings of an untrained man confronted by a scientific complexity.

Not for the first time he realized how much he actually needed Lesbee, or somebody like him.

But he knew also what had driven him. He wanted the captain's wives for himself; it was such a naked desire that had built up in him unbearably during this period when it seemed that he had lost everything.

Standing there, he accepted the partial defeat that was here.

"O.K., O.K.!" he said to his henchman in a savage tone, "we'll take the ship just like we did the first time—except we'll wait for the next sleep period and catch them by surprise. That gives us about ten hours. So let's get some sleep and be ready.

When the ten hours were up, his instructions were. "Kill only the Space Patrol guys—and Hewitt. We'll need the old ship people."

The attack on the ship led by Gourdy began as a movement of a straggling line of men traversing one deserted corridor after another. Presently, the first trio of men broke off from the main group and headed for the engine room. Two other segments of three soon turned off, one heading for the alternate control room, the other for the bridge. The main body of men accompanied Gourdy to the upper levels.

It was here in the first officer's apartment—according to Lesbee—that the Space Patrol headquarters had been established. Other patrol men occupied various adjoining cabins.

Two groups of three men were sent into that area with master keys and with instructions to attempt total surprise and show no mercy to any of the new men on the ship.

Gourdy and the remaining two men went cautiously on to the captain's cabin. Using another of the numerous keys Lesbee had made, Gourdy softly unlocked the outer door and tip-toed inside. . . . A minute later, two sleepy, startled women stared up at him from the beds in the master bedroom: his own wife, Marianne, and the woman, Ruth.

One of the other men had gone into the second bedroom. This individual now reported that it was occupied by Ilsa and Ann.

—No Hewitt. Never had been! Why hadn't Lesbee told him—?

Gourdy felt an intense but momentary rage. His emotion yielded to urgency. He left the women and headed for the detector instrument.

All the apartments he scanned were occupied.

After a few minutes of hastily searching for Hewitt, he realized that such a survey would take too long. As a final check, he switched to the dormitory in the lower part of the ship. It was deserted. So they were probably all back with their families.

He sought and found the button that flashed on the interior of patrol headquarters. It was a grimly satisfying scene: two dead men in pajamas. A woman lay sobbing on one of the bodies.

Flicking over to the cabins, one by one, he saw with total delight that his men had made a victorious sweep. . . . In two of the apartments there had been fighting, the surprise evidently not complete. In one room, one of his own henchmen lay dead. But across from him was a dead stranger.

These two cabins were in shambles.

Jubilant, rubbing his hands with his absolute joy, Gourdy stepped out into the main room. The two men were standing nervously out in the corridor; he could see them through the door. The four women had put on dressing gowns and stood in a tight little group near the door of the main bedroom.

His women. Soon.

"Well, ladies," he said, grinning widely, "looks like I'm going to be captain again."

Silence greeted his words. After a moment, the glum expressions on all four women's faces irritated him. "By God!" he said, "I'll kick you all out of here if you don't show a little interest!"

Tears came into Ruth's eyes. Then a sob escaped her lips. It was like a signal. All four women started to cry.

Gourdy went into an instant, towering rage. "Get into that room over there!" he ordered. He indicated the second bedroom. "And stay there."

The sobs subsided. Silent again, they went inside and closed the door.

The two men had entered the room while this interchange was going on. One asked nervously, "What's happening, Captain?"

"We're winning," said Gourdy.

But he hurried back to the detector instrument, to make sure.

With fumbling fingers, he tuned in on the engine room. There, also, was victory. Former First Officer Miller had been captured.

Gourdy broke in upon the scene via his viewplate communicator. Addressing Miller, he said, "Where's Hewitt?"

Miller was visibly in a state of shock but his answer sounded sincere: "In one of the cabins upstairs. I don't know which one—honest!"

Gourdy believed him. "We'll get him!" he said savagely. and broke the connection.

Unfortunately, there were well over a hundred apartments in the upper part of the ship. It disturbed Gourdy that somehow his luck hadn't enabled him to pick out the one Hewitt was in.

"Damn it!" he thought. "Why didn't he try to grab these women, like any normal man would do?"

These emotions subsided as, one by one, his men reported in person. It was victory all along the line.

"—Went into some wrong cabins!" Harcourt said. "Soon as we saw they were old ship folk, we told 'em—like you said—to just stay indoors and no funny stuff. . . . But some of them know now what's going on."

Almost all his followers made similar reports.

Gourdy was indifferent. "We know what those characters are like," he said contemptuously.

There was the musical sound of the intercom turning on, Gourdy automatically headed toward it. Abruptly, he stopped, frowned with amazement. "But *who* can be calling?" he said.

He was still scowling as he clicked on his end of the machine.

Hewitt!

The two men stared at each other's images, Gourdy's eyes narrowed, Hewitt's were grave. It was Hewitt who spoke.

"I've just been advised of your attempted take-over, Gourdy. I don't know how you got aboard but you've made the mistake of your life."

For Gourdy, one word stood out *"—Advised!—"*

He snarled, "Who advised you? Wait till I lay my hands on—"

Hewitt went on grimly, "And I've got a score of men already gathered, and more coming every minute—"

Gourdy felt his first chill.

"—We're armed!" said Hewitt. "And in a few minutes we're starting up there to get you, so you'd better surrender before it's too late."

Gourdy had recovered. "You won't get far with that gang of cowards!" he said scornfully, and he broke the connection.

39

The battle to recover the ship began about an hour later.

On one side were eighteen men armed with blasters, revolvers, and several shotguns. Opposing them were principally the scientists and technicians. They had blasters, revolvers, a number of gas guns, and equipment from their laboratories.

Gourdy kept believing that his opponents were cowards because once before they had allowed themselves to be imprisoned without trying to defend themselves. Hewitt knew that there was little truth to it. A new factor had been added. The old ship people now had the courage required of them by the system of which they had become a part during the past few weeks.

Hewitt had no doubt that these men were still profoundly prejudiced in connection with their women, and that they retained other narrow attitudes. But for each man, the prospect of once more being in the control of Gourdy and his gang was unthinkable.

Once that decision was made—and apparently it had been made instantly by many persons—there was no problem. Instinctively, they had turned to Hewitt. And when he requested them to come up with some ideas for the attack, the physics, chemistry, and engineering experts produced:

. . . A development of laser, where the light beam carried an electrical charge—

. . . An energy field affecting the nervous system, cramping certain muscles—

. . . A little round ball that rolled into the engine room, attached itself to one of the drives, sucked energy from it, and began to radiate heat. When the temperature in the engine room was 180 degrees Fahrenheit, the small group of Gourdy's men who were inside sent Miller out to ask if they could surrender.

Hewitt ordered that they be permitted to do so.

From the prisoners they learned for the first time of Lesbee's murder. Hewitt listened to the description the man gave of how everything had seemed to stand still while they were leaving the prison and of how this had also happened at certain other times. He recognized the similarity to his own experience when he originally came aboard the ship.

He became very excited. It seemed to him that a controlled method of mechanically altering time ratios would solve their entire space-time confusion.

But presently he realized that Gourdy's men would be no help. They had never grasped the meaning of what was happening to them.

A young scientist named Roscoe had a sudden bright thought: If Lesbee had returned to the ship, then Tellier must be back also. Hewitt dispatched the young man with a patrol to search the lifeboats. And there, indeed, was Tellier.

But he could only weep when told of Lesbee's death. His knowledge of Lesbee's ideas was sketchy, almost valueless.

In strict meaning, what the scientists did now was not new. None of the devices that were mobilized for battle was an original invention of anyone aboard the *Hope of Man*. Each was a known process. However, it took an expert to utilize it.

For the scientists, the struggle was like a game. They had scores of devices and processes—

Gourdy's man on the bridge was requested to surrender. He refused to do so. Whereupon, a speaker inside the bridge control board began to give forth a sound. It was an all-range speaker. And so the sound presently became so intense that it threatened to rupture the eardrums of the man.

By the time he surrendered, the two men in the auxiliary control room were being subjected to flames that broke right out of the walls. It was actually a laser phenomenon, whereby a mixture of many light waves—including a few in the heat band—were evoked from metal crystals in the walls. The flame-like tongues of flickering light reached out ten and twenty feet, randomly, without warning. They were far from being as hot as fire, but there was heat from them, and this created the psychological effect of fire. After a few minutes, Gourdy's henchman came rushing out to surrender.

The man who reported this particular success to Hewitt, added in disgust: "What gripes me is, we could have fought that gang with this stuff the first time they took over—"

Hewitt stared at the man, who was almost as big a fellow as Harcourt, but older, and for a moment he was minded to let the remark pass.

But his mind flashed back to the similar situation on Earth. There, also, tens of thousands of scientists were the only people who as a group understood and could utilize the forces of nature. Yet, even under a dictatorship, it had been observed that this vast group of knowledgeable people had no system by which they could emerge from their laboratories and utilize their training for any other purpose than what was dictated to them from above.

Remembering this, Hewitt shook his head at the scientist, whose name was William Lawrence. "I disagree," he said. "For a hundred years, you people were not politically minded. The successive rulers of the ship saw to that. Now you are." He smiled, tight-lipped. "Feels different, doesn't it?"

The end of the designated sleep period drew near. Large groups of men had gradually taken up positions at all approaches to the captain's cabin. And the question of what the nature of the attack should be was essentially limited only by consideration for the captain's wives.

Led by Lawrence, a group of scientists came to Hewitt. Their spokesman said earnestly, "I'm afraid we're going to have to sacrifice those women. Otherwise, it may be a case of a direct physical assault. We may lose thirty or forty men."

The possibility had already been weighing on Hewitt. Now, he broached the subject of persuading Gourdy to surrender with a promise of no punishment.

"After all those people he's killed!" Several voices uttered similar sentiments in tones that were loud with outrage.

Hewitt felt a sharp anger. Because if a compromise were justified at all, it should include saving everyone, if possible. He said, "Gourdy killed those men for personal political reasons."

"It was murder!" said Lawrence harshly.

Holding his irritation, Hewitt explained that on some level the charge was true. Killing was killing. But until comparatively recent times, the system accepted by the masses of the people, held political leaders in a special category. And *real* change on that point was probably still a long way off. This was a truth which people emerging into a new system were not clearly aware of.

Hewitt said, "We could almost determine the nature of a

society by the kind of killing it permits and justifies. And when we look at who in that society is responsible for the administration of death and other penalties, we see that the killers have the sanction of the political leaders who, in turn, have broad mass support for their actions."

He continued, "Here on the ship you've had a somewhat telescoped version of all this. And now that you're in a transition from one system to another, you can't bring yourself to tolerate the particular violence that was part of the old system. If there's anyone here who actively opposed the old system, I'll be glad to hear what he has to say."

There was a long silence, and then former First Officer Miller raised his hand. "I opposed the old system," he said.

One of the scientists made a sputtering sound, and then said in a tone of muffled anger, "Mr. Miller, I cannot accept that statement without evidence."

"I hated this guy Gourdy's guts from the moment I saw him," said Miller indignantly.

"What about your blankety-blank guts when you were Browne's lackey?" said the scientist in a thick voice.

Miller looked surprised. "Mr. Browne was the lawful captain of this ship!" he protested.

Hewitt waved the two men to silence. Then, smiling faintly, he faced the group. "You see what I mean," he said.

The young scientist, Roscoe, muttered, "I don't really get it. But I have a feeling it's there. All right, so you promise him immunity. What are you going to do with the so-and-so after that?"

"Fit him into the new system," said Hewitt frankly.

"Suppose he won't fit?"

"I'm willing to take the chance," said Hewitt. "Now, is it all right if I try to deal with him?"

Several men shifted their gazes when he looked directly at them but there was no vocal opposition.

Gourdy laughed uproariously when Hewitt called him. "Look," he said, "we're down to the stuff that separates the men from the boys. And you've got the boys and I've got the men. With the supplies we have in the connecting storerooms, we can hold out for years."

Hewitt suggested that the scientific potentialities available to the attackers would be decisive. He finished, "So I can only assume that you don't trust my offer. Is that it?"

"Sure, I trust it."

"Then what is it?" Hewitt persisted. "If you don't accept this offer, it's the end of the road, Gourdy."

"I still think I'm going to win," Gourdy replied. "That scientific stuff—you know damn well the previous captains made sure that none of that could affect the captain's cabin."

Hewitt explained: "They made sure of it by having the scientific people on their side."

The image of Gourdy in the viewplate merely shrugged scornfully.

But he was shaken, in spite of himself.

At some depth of his being, he believed that this was the end. Yet he could not bring himself to acknowledge it. Something might still happen. What? He had no idea. But surrender remained unthinkable.

Hewitt said in a steady voice, "You can surrender on my offer at any time before the first shots are fired!" With that he broke the connection.

Several scientists had stood by during Hewitt's interchange with Gourdy. Now, one of them said, "From the look on your face, you don't seem quite so objective."

"Gourdy is getting harder to like," Hewitt confessed. "But I assume he's under tension, too."

But he grew calmer as he had his tank wheeled out and explained what he had in mind. When he had been sealed into it, he gave the signal for action. Whereupon he guided his suit toward the corridor that led to the captain's cabin.

The first bullet struck the ultra-hard plastic directly in front of his eyes! It distorted, then normalized. Hewitt pulled back, a tremor shaking his body.

But he recovered, and continued to guide his machine forward.

A line of sparks the size of marbles seemed to run down the full frontal length of the suit—a blaster! The effect wa so eerie that he was more fascinated than startled.

A blast from a shotgun also struck him head on. The noise of it was momentarily stunning.

But it was an undamaged Hewitt that drove forward. As he came within yards of the entrance, he heard Gourdy's voice from beyond the door: "Damn you, Hewitt, what do you want?"

"I want to talk."

"You can talk on the intercom."

"Face to face is better."

There was a pause. "All right, come on in!"

Once more, Hewitt moved forward, keenly aware that his advisers and he had analyzed that Gourdy's strong-arm men would try to tip the tank suit the moment he drove it into the room. It would not be easy to do. The suit itself weighed nearly 450 pounds at one g, and he himself added 190 to that. Yet three or four men could undoubtedly knock it over.

So he stopped in the doorway, where they would not be able to get at him. And because he had the simple purpose of saving the women, he ignored the men and his gaze flashed toward the bedroom doors.

Miraculously, after a moment, the door of one bedroom opened slightly. Through the slit, a bright eye peered at him. Who it was he could not make out.

Hewitt didn't wait to find out any more. He started forward with a jerk. At its top speed of ten miles an hour, his vehicle moved across the room. He was vaguely aware of men jumping at him with reaching hands. Their yells of dismay as they touched the suit's electrical field was not an unpleasant sound in his ears.

As he approached the door of the bedroom, Hewitt spoke through his speaker: "Ladies, get out of the way!"

Moments later, the nose of the vehicle struck the door with enough impact to have smashed it if it had been closed. But it was ajar. And so the door bounced open, with a bang. Hewitt rolled through. The instant he was inside he saw that all four women were there.

He felt greatly relieved, for he had two signals for this moment.

He spoke into his mike: "Fire!"

That was the word that indicated that he was in a position to protect all the women.

The response from the scientists was immediate. Jagged lightning arced from a concentration point in the wall, struck the suit, and discharged from its rear into the main room behind him.

From that room came a screaming of men in agony. Then Hewitt heard the thud of one body after another falling to the floor like deadweights.

40

Hewitt called into his mike, "You'd better get up here quick!"

"No hurry," was the cool reply. "They won't be bothering anybody again."

The voice was that of William Lawrence, and his tone was so suggestive that Hewitt was startled. Without another word, suddenly uneasy, he backed up, turned around, and drove out into the main room.

A dozen men lay sprawled in various positions on the floor.

There was something about the way the bodies lay—so still—that chilled Hewitt. "Lawrence," Hewitt said into his mike, and his voice had a high-pitched quality, "the agreement was—"

Lawrence's voice in his earphones had a grim chuckle in it. "I'm afraid, Mr. Hewitt, that quite accidentally we gave them a lethal dosage. Too bad."

Rage surged through Hewitt, as much as the tone of voice as at the meaning. He yelled, "You're just another murderer!"

Lawrence was cool. "You're overexcited, Mr. Hewitt. But it's all right. We won't hold anything you say right now against you."

Hewitt fought for self-control. But his next words still had bitterness in them. "I suppose what you've done has its good side," he said. "Just as you unthinkingly conformed to the old system, so now you're unthinkingly responding to the new one."

"You don't think we were going to let him get away!" said Lawrence, suddenly angry, his voice high-pitched.

"All right, all right," Hewitt soothed. "Let's clean up and go to sleep. I'm exhausted."

He had caught a glimpse of a woman in the doorway behind him. He activated his speaker. "Ladies," he commanded, "stay in that bedroom and close the door, please!"

167

A moment later, the door shut softly, but not before he heard someone start to sob.

Hewitt was awakened by the ringing of his door buzzer. Hastily, he slipped into his robe and opened the door. The visitor who stood outside in the corridor was Roscoe, the young scientist.

"We're gathering in the main assembly room, sir," Roscoe said, "and we want you there. Men only."

Hewitt stared at him, his smile fading. But all he said was, "I'll be there in ten minutes."

He shaved and dressed hurriedly, partly resigned to the implications of Roscoe's words. It was possible that what could be done swiftly on the ship was done. The rest would require education over a period of time, and the interaction of many people, who had yet to become aware of all of the potentialities of the new system.

. . . He had set up a self-perpetuating program. In such a framework, each person was motivated in a strict, selfish way to maintain the frame. Such a system had flexibility. It didn't, for instance, need a particular moral code or a particular leader. That was what he now faced, a people who were free to do as they wanted.

As Hewitt appeared in the doorway of the assembly hall, several people saw him. A man leaped to his feet, yelled: "Here he is!"

It was an unexpected greeting. On hearing the words, Hewitt stopped.

As he stood there, uncertain, the several hundred men in the hall rose to their feet and, to his amazement, cheered him wildly. He grew aware that William Lawrence, a broad grin on his face, was on the stage . . . waving for him to come forward.

Hewitt walked forward gingerly. He sensed that he was by no means out of trouble, but he was beginning to feel a lot better.

As soon as Hewitt was on the stage, Lawrence held up a hand for silence. When he had it, he addressed Hewitt in a loud, clear voice.

"Mr. Hewitt, as you may have gathered, you have only friends here. The way you came aboard, the system you set up, your motives for all that you have done, have convinced us that you operate from the highest ethical considerations. For these and other reasons, this assembly wishes to go on record as saying that it believes you to be the natural leader of this expedition."

He had to pause, to wave down an audience that began to clap and yell. When he had silence once more, he continued.

"However, there are special problems in running this ship, and before we accept you as captain, we want to make certain that you don't interfere in areas that are no concern of yours. Mr. Hewitt, this assembly would like to inquire, what are you going to do with the captain's wives?"

The switch from the general to the particular came so swiftly that Hewitt stood blank for a moment. It took a few moments longer for him to grasp that he was actually being asked a direct question on such a matter.

Slowly, he walked forward, and it was evident to him that a great deal depended on his answer. He wondered if he could back down from truth. He could not.

"Gentlemen," he said, "I don't know how long we shall continue out here in space. But I'm assuming that considerable time will go by while we do experiment, research, and correlation of data in the vast laboratory of the space-time continuum. Naturally, the human life aboard must and will go on in human terms during that period. There will be marriages, the births of children, educational programs, and other important matters."

He stopped, suddenly embarrassed. What he had to say was not for a roomful of men in an auditorium. Nonetheless, after a moment, he went on firmly.

"I feel a strong attraction for the oldest of the four women you refer to, and I hope she feels the same for me. It is my intention to ask her to marry me."

Something of his profound sincerity must have penetrated to his listeners as he spoke the simply words. For, after he had finished, there was dead silence. On the platform, William Lawrence stroked his jaw and looked at the floor.

It was Roscoe who stood up. "Mr. Hewitt," he said, "during all my life and all my father's life, the captain of the *Hope of Man* has been a man with more than one wife. Are you telling us that you are going to change this, that you are going to limit yourself to one wife?"

Hewitt stood quietly staring out at an audience that had remained silent and expectant. Everybody seemed to be gazing at him intently. He felt it was ridiculous, that these foolish men were going to try to hold him to the tradition of more than one wife. He surmised that conforming would be proof to them that he would maintain male hegemony aboard the *Hope of Man*.

Whatever their motive, he rejected the reasoning behind it, and he said, "Yes—one wife."

All over the auditorium, grins suddenly showed on the upturned faces.

Then Lawrence came over and shook Hewitt's hand.

From the floor, Roscoe said, "Well, Captain Hewitt, you've passed out tests. We're for you. We'll trust you. Right, men?"

Hewitt received his second ovation.

41

Eight years went by on the ship.

The scientists aboard learned by trial and error what John Lesbee V had divined in a flash of insight. But they rejected his description of it. The universe was not a "lie." It was what it was. There had been an "apparency" perceived by the highly evolved nervous systems of man and animals. Evidently—it was postulated—life had required a unique stability and had therefore *created* brain mechanisms that limited perception to the apparent stable condition. Within this "solid" frame, life lived its lulled existence, evolving painfully, constantly adjusting at some unconscious level to the real universe.

And so here was man, through his scientifically trained senses, able to examine the truth at last.

. . . They measured that truth, discovered basic principles, made predictions, verified them. Control of time was achieved through a gradational, mechanical manipulation of the light-speed conditions.

Originally, the *Hope of Man* had slipped back in time accidentally. Now, the great ship was manipulated through the timeless universe of translight-speeds.

Although over four hundred weeks had gone by aboard, it came to a one-to-one ratio in the solar system one week, Earth time, after the *Molly D* had cast loose and started back to Earth.

The two vessels went into orbit around the planet within a day of each other. For the salvage ship, seven days had gone by; for the interstellar ship, nearly three thousand days—

There followed an emergency meeting of the cabinet, consultation with the Asian bloc, and widespread intercommunication among scientists.

Then, and not till then, Peter Linden and Averill Hewitt addressed the world.

The physicist spoke first and gave the scientific information. In sum, this was: the *Hope of Man* had gone into the future of the solar system and had observed the sun briefly assume some of the characteristics of a Cepheid Variable.

As he made these statements, the television showed motion pictures of that future event: the sudden flare-up, the heat waves striking one side of the Earth—

The scientist was careful to explain many times that what they were seeing on their television was something that had actually been photographed in the future. It was—or would be when it happened—the result of a translight-speed condition of basic matter. Moving faster than light, on a front of many light-years, this condition—which resembled in shape a ripple in space—would shortly envelop the solar system.

Traveling faster than light, the ripple would pass through the sun in about four seconds and would traverse the ninety-three million miles from the sun to Earth in six and a half minutes.

All the damage would be caused by the heat transported by the ripple from its four-second contact with the sun.

"Mercury," said Peter Linden, "will be horribly scorched, "but all the planets, including Earth, will survive."

Nevertheless, shelters must be dug. During the period of flare-up, the people on the side of the Earth exposed to the sun must be underground. . . . Fortunately, the huge Pacific Ocean would bear the brunt—

When his turn came before the cameras and microphones, Hewitt said, "I have happier news."

During its period of translight-speed cruising, the *Hope of Man* had visited scores of other sun systems. They had found three other available planets that men could live on. Many colonists were needed to augment those who were already there.

"Right now," said Hewitt, "my own family—my wife, Ruth, and our four children—are on one of those planets. It will be our permanent home."

Those words were the beginning of the sales talk he made as the world listened in.

BOOKS

Presenting JOHN NORMAN in DAW editions . . .

☐ **HUNTERS OF GOR**   (#UE1472—$2.25)

☐ **MARAUDERS OF GOR**   (#UE1465—$2.25)

☐ **TRIBESMEN OF GOR**   (#UE1473—$2.25)

☐ **SLAVE GIRL OF GOR**   (#UE1474—$2.25)

☐ **BEASTS OF GOR**   (#UE1471—$2.25)

☐ **EXPLORERS OF GOR**   (#UE1449—$2.25)

☐ **FIGHTING SLAVE OF GOR**   (#UE1522—$2.25)

☐ **TIME SLAVE**   (#UJ1322—$1.95)

☐ **IMAGINATIVE SEX**   (#UE1546—$2.25)

☐ **GHOST DANCE**   (#UE1501—$2.25)

With two and a half million copies of DAW's John
Norman books in print, these enthralling novels
are in constant demand. They combine heroic ad-
venture, interplanetary peril, and the in-depth de-
piction of Earth's counter-orbital twin with a special
talent all of their own.

But be warned—they are addictive!

If you wish to order these titles,

please use the coupon on

the last page of this book.

Attention:

DAW COLLECTORS

Many readers of DAW Books have written requesting information on early titles and book numbers to assist in the collection of DAW editions since the first of our titles appeared in April 1972.

We have prepared a several-pages-long list of all DAW titles, giving their sequence numbers, original and current order numbers, and ISBN numbers. And of course the authors and book titles, as well as reissues.

If you think that this list will be of help, you may have a copy by writing to the address below and enclosing fifty cents in stamps or coins to cover the handling and postage costs.

DAW BOOKS, INC.   Dept. C
1633 Broadway
New York, N.Y. 10019

DRAY PRESCOT

The great Novels of Kregen, world of Antares

Fully illustrated

If you wish to order these titles,
please use the coupon on
the last page of this book.

DAW sf BOOKS

A. E. VAN VOGT
in DAW Editions: